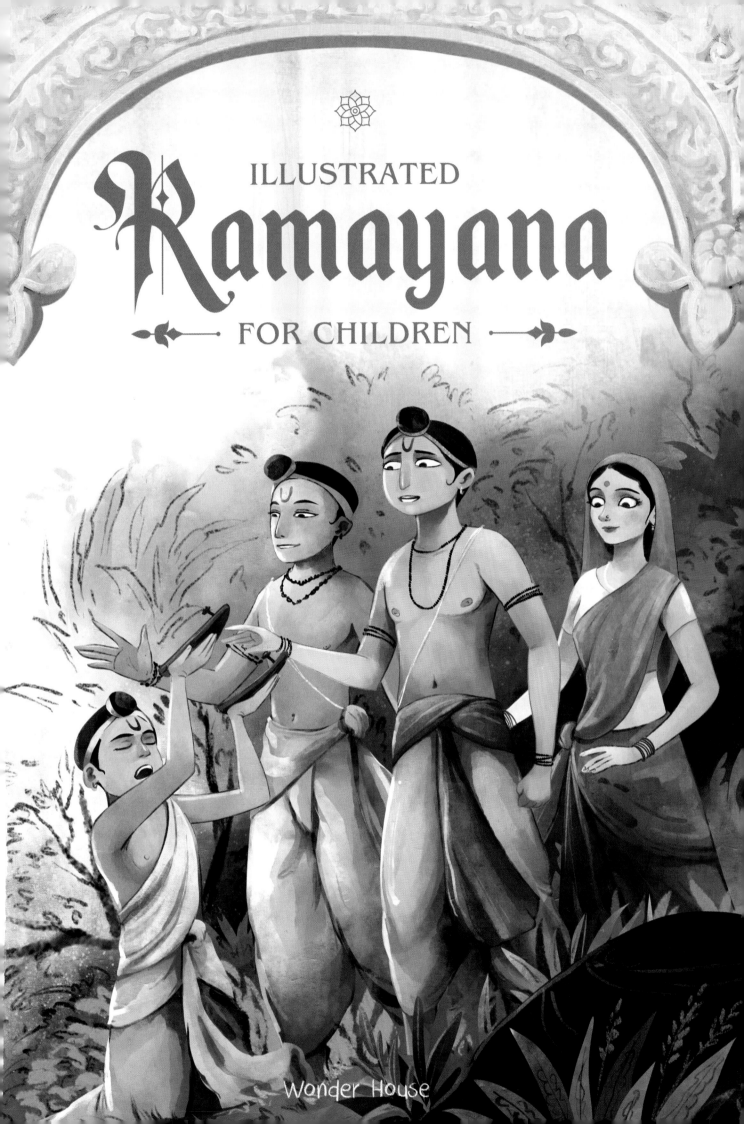

Wonder House

(An imprint of Prakash Books)

contact@wonderhousebooks.com

ISBN : 978-93-90391-59-2

❀ About the Author ❀

Shubha Vilas is a storyteller, motivational speaker and an author, who holds a degree in engineering and patent law, but he chose to leave the mainstream society to live a life of contemplation, and study scripture in depth.

As a child, his grandmother regaled him with stories from the Ramayana, which captured his heart and soul, and thus began his tryst with scriptures. He started writing stories inspired by the Ramayana and how it is still as relevant to us as it was in the Treta yuga.

Some of his popular works include *Open Eyed Meditations*, and *Mystical Tales for A Magical Life: 11 Unheard Fantastic Vedic Stories* which transform Vedic literature and epics into relatable stories and contemporary life lessons. Shubha has penned down a fun-filled version of Panchatantra stories for children titled *Pandit Vishnu Sharma's Panchatantra: Illustrated Tales from Ancient India*, to captivate them with beautiful illustrations, and lessons that sharpen their thinking abilities.

Shubha is deeply passionate about imparting education that helps build character in children. This has led him to create a value-education module which can be incorporated into children's existing syllabi. With this module, he guides young minds towards an inspiring life, filled with values and principles.

Contents

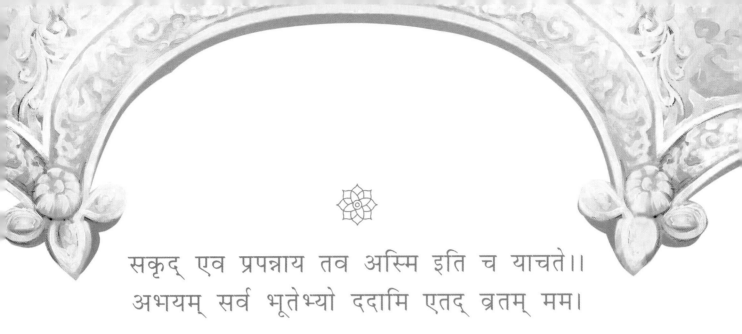

सकृद् एव प्रपन्नाय तव अस्मि इति च याचते।।
अभयम् सर्व भूतेभ्यो ददामि एतद् व्रतम् मम।

– Valmiki Ramayana, Yuddha Kanda 6.18.33

"Whoever takes shelter in me, having said 'I am yours' just once, I vow
to protect them and grant them fearlessness."

Rama proclaims this when the Vanaras report Vibhishan's desire to
take his shelter.

Characters

Dasharatha

King of Ayodhya and father of Rama, Laxman, Bharat and Shatrughana. His name alludes to the fact that his chariot could simultaneously fly in ten different directions.

Rama

Beloved prince and eventual king of Ayodhya who established Rama-rajya on the principles of justice and prosperity for all. He built a bridge to Lanka to save his kidnapped wife Sita from Ravana.

Laxman

Rama's brother who was always at his side, even during 14 long years of exile

Sita

Adopted daughter of King Janak of Mithila, she is said to have been found in a ditch in the earth. Rama won her hand in marriage after breaking Shiva's bow in a swayamvar.

Vashishtha

One of the most respected sages, he is the spiritual advisor of the Ikshvaku dynasty and guru of Rama.

Ravana

The demonic king of Lanka who was so powerful that he even conquered gods and ruled over them. His pride made him kidnap Sita and he was eventually killed by Rama.

Hanuman

A Vanara who was so powerful that he swallowed the sun as a baby. A devotee of Lord Rama, he played the most important role in the war against Ravana.

Vibhishan

Brother of Ravana, but saintly in qualities. He took Lord Rama's shelter and revealed his brother's secrets, which helped Rama kill Ravana.

Joy in Ayodhya

The solar dynasty, one of the oldest families of India, is so old that the sun god Surya is their original ancestor. King Dasharatha belonged to this dynasty and ruled the kingdom of Kosala. But all his wealth could not buy him happiness. The happiness of having a child. And so, King Dasharatha lived a sad life.

One day, Guru Vashishtha suggested that he organise a sacrifice to please the gods, who would then bless him with a child. With the blessings of his guru, King Dasharatha successfully completed the grandest of all sacrifices The fire blazing from the sacrifice was sky-high, prompting the demigods to step down and accept the offerings. Soon after that, a celestial being appeared.

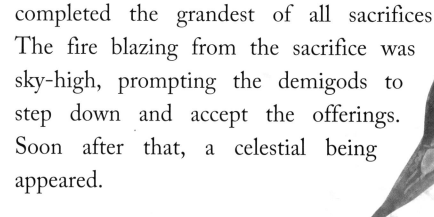

King Dasharatha was super excited. Although he was 60,000 years old, he had never felt younger. Standing before him was a divine being sent from the higher planets to fulfil his long-cherished dream of becoming a father. The mountainous figure was dressed in red and black, with a mane like that of a lion. Decorated with ornaments, he appeared as effulgent as the sun. He held in his hand a golden pot that dazzled more than him. It was so precious that he kept it close to his heart and approached the euphoric king. Dasharatha felt tingling excitement as he stood nervously, like a small child waiting for a sweet.

In a thumping voice, the celestial being informed King Dasharatha that the sacrifice had been successful. Handing over the radiant pot to the nervous king, he said, "Divide this nectar among your three queens." And he disappeared as quickly as he had appeared.

King Dasharatha felt like he had received the wealth of the entire world. He was holding not nectar, but all his hopes and dreams. He gave half of it to Kaushalya, his first wife, who drank it immediately. A quarter went to Keikeyi, his most beautiful wife, who also drank it eagerly. Half of the remainder he gave to Sumitra. Being extremely virtuous and pious, Sumitra held the heavenly potion in her hands prayerfully. There was still some nectar in the pot and after much deliberation, the king gave it to Sumitra. Filled with gratitude, Sumitra poured the double portions into her mouth, savouring the unique manna.

As soon as the three queens devoured the nectar, their bodies began to glow. And they continued to glow for 12 months, till it was time to give birth. After 12 months, the three queens would finally fulfil the king's dreams.

The first to give birth was Kaushalya, in the month of Chaitra (April), on the ninth day of the waxing moon, at noon. Dasharatha nearly fainted with excitement when he saw the baby, soft as a petal, none other than the Lord himself. He was totally mesmerised by the baby's moonlike face, lotus eyes, and rounded cheeks. And would you believe it? A light green translucent body! The world around him melted when he held the baby dearly in his arms. He was transported to another world where nothing else existed, only him and his precious baby.

The next morning, Keikeyi gave birth to her child. And by noon, Sumitra was a mother of twins! (Remember she had consumed two portions of the nectar?)

Nothing could stop the people of Ayodhya from celebrating now, for they were welcoming the arrival of not one but four princes! Never had they experienced so much joy, so much fulfilment and so much peace. They sang, they danced, they showered flowers on each other. King Dasharatha, in turn, announced that there would be no tax collection for seven years. He opened his treasury to all, giving away gems and jewels as gifts. For King Dasharatha, celebration meant making his subjects happy. Distributing joy was a sure way of welcoming auspiciousness.

On the eleventh day, Sage Vashishtha came to the palace for the naming ceremony. "Rama!" The name sprung to his lips when he saw Kaushalya's son. Rama means one who gives pleasure. Did he not give pleasure to not just one family, but to every family in the vast kingdom of Ayodhya? Keikeyi's son was named Bharat, one who has a big burden on his head, or rather, one who has infinite capacity to take responsibility of a heavy burden, without thinking of himself.

Sumitra's twins were named Laxman and Shatrughana. Laxman comes from the root word, Laxmi, which means wealth. Laxman desired not money, but the wealth of being of service to Rama. And Shatrughana means one who conquers enemies.

One day, the four children were crying in their cradles. Their cries had brought the entire palace to a standstill. The mothers tried everything to pacify them, but no one could decipher why the four were continuously crying together. Finally, Sage Vashishtha was called to help them out.

The sage came and surveyed the situation. Rama was in one cradle, Bharat in another; Laxman next to them them, followed by Shatrughana in the last cradle. The wise sage shuffled the cradles so that Laxman's cradle was next to Rama's and Bharat's cradle was next to Shatrughana's.

As soon as he did this, the crying abated. However, they were still crying! So, he lifted Laxman and put him in Rama's cradle. Similarly, he lifted Shatrughana and put him in Bharat's cradle. The children clung to each other and started smiling. Everyone was shocked to see the love between the brothers. Such a beautiful bond! The mothers continued to use this magical formula whenever the kids cried.

Growing up, Rama and Laxman were inseparable, as were Bharat and Shatrughana. Rama refused to eat or sleep unless Laxman was there. And whenever Rama went somewhere, Laxman ran behind him. Soon, it was time to enrol them in Sage Vashishtha's ashram for their schooling. King Dasharatha went and dropped them there with a heavy heart.

The four boys began learning the basics. Rama was such a natural with his bow and arrow that they seemed like an extension of his limbs. He could also ride elephants, horses and chariots with great expertise. He put in his heart and soul in learning whatever was being taught to him. The brothers frequently visited sages and sat at their feet, learning the scriptures. Their goal was to ultimately serve society to the best of their abilities.

The Pain of Separation

Dasharatha couldn't believe his ears! Had he heard correctly? Was something wrong with his ears? Was the great Sage Vishwamitra really asking him to give away his life, his soul—his son Rama? He stared at Vishwamitra with his mouth open! It all began when the guard came running into his court, frightened to death. Someone on the door had threatened to burn him to ashes if he was not allowed to enter. He called himself Vishwamitra. Could it be the Sage Vishwamitra?

King Dasharatha and his ministers rushed to greet the sage. They brought him inside with great respect and a grand reception.

Dasharatha welcomed the sage with pleasing words, "Your footsteps in my kingdom have purified this land. Please tell me the purpose of your visit and I will fulfil your desire."

Vishwamitra, as his name suggested, was a friend for the entire world. He was conducting a big fire sacrifice to please God, only for the benefit of mankind. But he was unable to complete it, thanks to two ferocious and shape-shifting demons—Maricha and Subahu. They cleverly threw flesh and blood into the fire, which polluted the sacrifice. And Vishwamitra would have to start from the beginning. They harassed Vishwamitra and obstructed his goal in this manner. He lamented, "I have come to ask you for shelter, King Dasharatha. Please give me your son Rama to guard the sacrifice from the two demons. You have already promised to fulfil my desire."

Dasharatha's jaw dropped. His world exploded. He saw Yamaraj in front of him, as if taking away his life. He had been blessed with a child after years of waiting. Rama was hardly 12 years old. And this sage wanted to take him away? To fight demons? How would a little boy do that? Maricha and Subahu were extremely wicked!

Trying to bargain, he said, "I will give you my entire army to fight the demons. I myself will come, but I beg you, please don't ask for Rama!"

Dasharatha knew his son better than Vishwamitra. He was a delicate child. Not a demon killer. He could barely stay awake after sunset! Fighting nocturnal demons would be impossible.

He fell at Vishwamitra's feet, begging to go along with him instead, "I have prayed and struggled for 60,000 years to get Rama. How can I let him go? At least let me accompany him along with my army!"

Now, Vishwamitra was really angry. He had reached his boiling point. The entire courtroom was burning with the fire blazing in his red eyes.

Sage Vashishtha, who had been silent till now, decided it was time for him to speak. Looking at King Dasharatha, he said, "Never before have you gone back on your word. You come from the great dynasty of Ikshvaku, who never violated any principles. It is now time to let go of Rama so he can grow. Like a river flows into an ocean, Rama will flow from Ayodhya to the vast ocean of Vishwamitra's knowledge.

I assure you, Rama will be safe with him. Lord Shiva himself has gifted him powerful weapons."

Dasharatha reluctantly accepted that he had to listen to Guru Vashishtha, because he was right. He agreed to Vishwamitra's demand for the greater benefit of society. Along with Rama, he also handed over Laxman, knowing that the two brothers were inseparable.

The brothers happily followed Vishwamitra out of Ayodhya, excited to go on a new adventure. They thought that fighting with demons would be fun! They couldn't have asked for more. But for Dasharatha, his life itself had departed. He had given his bundle of joy to someone else. But in his heart, he knew that Rama and Laxman would both be safe and back soon.

Rama Saves the Day

"What's this?" wondered Rama aloud on hearing a thundering sound. It seemed that it was coming from under the river. Rama, Laxman and Sage Vishwamitra were on a boat, crossing River Ganga. Meandering through fields and forests, Sage Vishwamitra had told them many stories. The hermitage they had halted at the previous night belonged to disciples of Lord Shiva and it was here that he had once burnt Kaamadeva (the Indian equivalent of Cupid, god of love) to ashes. Why? For shooting arrows of love while he was meditating!

Swooosh! Swoosh! There it was again. Rama looked at Vishwamitra. Vishwamitra explained, "Right now, we are at the confluence of Ganga and Sarayu, which is the source of this sound."

After reaching the southern end of Ganga, the team continued their journey on foot. They passed a dry, barren forest, which looked very out of place.

Vishwamitra explained that it was once a lush green patch of woodland where sages enjoyed meditating. But a demon called Sunda could not tolerate this. When Sunda refused to leave them in peace, Agastya, a very powerful sage, burnt him down.

All this was fascinating for Rama and Laxman, who were amazed at the power of the sages.

Vishwamitra continued with the story.

"Sunda's wife Tataka, along with her two sons Maricha and Subahu, naturally wanted revenge. Agastya also cursed them to become man-eating demons. In vengeance, Tataka burnt the forest completely and it became the deserted barren land that it is now. Maricha and Subahu then took shelter of Ravana.

And now, I depend on you and Laxman to save the sacrifice from the deadly trio of Tataka, Maricha and Subahu." Vishwamitra brought Rama's attention back to the present. He knew that Rama could easily kill the trio but he also knew what could stop him. Rama would hesitate to kill a demoness, because he worshipped every woman like a mother. His respect for women would not allow him to kill a demoness. So, Vishwamitra told Rama what kind of a woman she was. "Tataka is not worthy of respect. She is a monster. Even the demigods are scared of her acts of terrorism. As and when necessary, evil beings have to be killed, whether men or women. It is your duty to carry out such missions to protect the innocent, even if it appears ruthless or sinful."

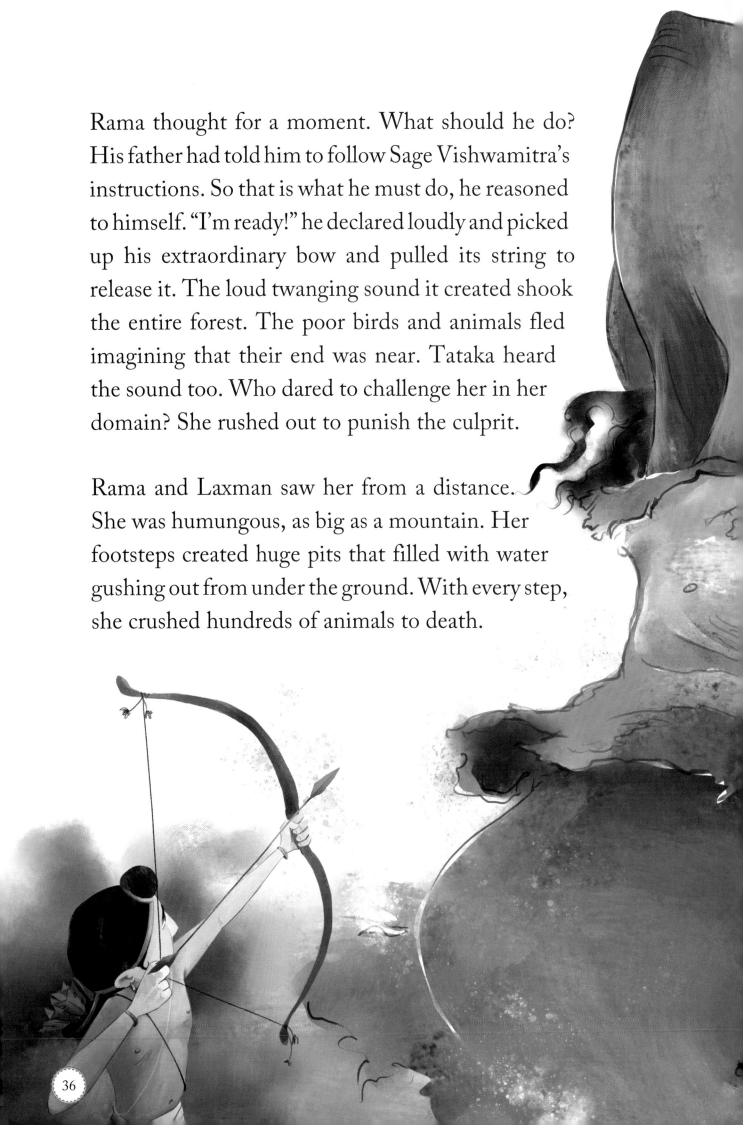

Rama thought for a moment. What should he do? His father had told him to follow Sage Vishwamitra's instructions. So that is what he must do, he reasoned to himself. "I'm ready!" he declared loudly and picked up his extraordinary bow and pulled its string to release it. The loud twanging sound it created shook the entire forest. The poor birds and animals fled imagining that their end was near. Tataka heard the sound too. Who dared to challenge her in her domain? She rushed out to punish the culprit.

Rama and Laxman saw her from a distance. She was humungous, as big as a mountain. Her footsteps created huge pits that filled with water gushing out from under the ground. With every step, she crushed hundreds of animals to death.

Was this really a woman? As she came closer, her garland became visible. It was not made of flowers, but elephants. The trunk of one elephant was tied to the tail of another! This elephant garland was around her neck. Her ears were studded with elephant heads. Her teeth resembled the trident of Yamaraj, the god of death.

She was like a tornado approaching Rama. But he stood calmly with his bow and aimed an arrow at her. His hand faltered, uneasy at the thought of killing a woman. He decided to simply maim her instead of killing her.

But that was a mistake. She hid from Rama's view and hurled huge rocks at both Rama and Laxman.

Vishwamitra, guessing Rama's intentions, warned the duo that her powers would increase enormously once the sun set. The time to kill her was now. His voice carried such urgency that Rama realised his mistake. Just then, Tataka laughed at his folly. Rama now knew where she was hiding. He shot an arrow in that direction and that was the end of Tataka. She fell to the ground in a huge pile of flesh. As soon as Tataka fell, the universe celebrated and the forest returned to its original glory.

With Tataka gone, everyone relaxed. Now the sacrifice began. Rama and Laxman had to watch out for Maricha and Subahu, who could attack from any direction, day or night. The two boys were like two eyes, alert and watchful. Six days passed under the vigil of Rama and Laxman, without any danger to the sacrifice.

It was the last phase of the sacrifice, with flames reaching the sky. All the sages were glowing, anticipating success, when all of a sudden, they heard a loud shriek from above. Maricha and Subahu were not alone. There were thousands of demons with them, each with four fangs and eyes emitting fire. They covered the area with spurious clouds that rained blood. Along with blood, they showered arrows, spears and other weapons on the sages. Not only that, they also uttered foul words from their foul mouths.

They could not actually descend because of the pious mantras chanted by the sages. They remained suspended in mid-air.

With one deadly arrow, Rama flung Maricha 800 miles away into the ocean. Another arrow and Subahu burst into flames instantly, reduced to nothing but ashes. Immediately, the clouds disappeared, giving way to soothing sunshine. The sacrifice was over and what a success it was! Without Rama and Laxman, it would have been impossible. Vishwamitra heaved a sigh of relief.

Rama asked his guru if there was anything else they could do for him. Vishwamitra happily asked them to accompany him to Mithila, where a yagya was organised by King Janak. The biggest attraction of the event was Shiva's bow. What was so special about it? They had heard about the famous bow, which was so heavy that it was impossible to lift. Even gods and demons were unable to lift and string it. Lord Shiva had given away his bow to celestial beings and then it had been passed on to a king as a reward. And finally, it had reached Mithila, where it was kept with great care and respect.

This was too good an opportunity to miss! They agreed to go to Mithila and continue their adventure.

4

More Adventures

There was no water in the river. What was flowing was sugarcane juice and honey! Not wanting to be left behind, the golden mangoes hanging from trees on the bank also sprayed their juice into the flowing river. Where were they? Had they died and reached heaven? The boys had many questions. Vishwamitra smiled and revealed that they were in the countryside of Mithila. But before going to Mithila, Vishwamitra wanted to show them something else. It was a broken-down hut that had seen better days. "The story goes back to Lord Brahma, who created a daughter called Ahalya from his imagination. He made sure that there was no one as beautiful as her, his most fascinating creation! But who was qualified enough to marry her? All the demigods wished for her hand, ready to do anything for her.

So, Brahma chalked out a competition. The fastest one to circumambulate the entire universe would be the winner and marry Ahalya. Amongst the contestants were Lord Indra and the wise Sage Gautam. To fulfil the challenge, he simply went around a cow, because mother cow represented the entire universe. He was thus declared the winner. Brahma was delighted to have such a wise son-in-law."

"Ahalya and Gautam lived in this very hut after they were married. Meanwhile, Indra was frothing with anger at having been denied a wife as beautiful as Ahalya. One day, he came to the couple's hut disguised as Sage Gautam, knowing that the sage had gone to bathe at the river. Ahalya did not notice the difference and let him enter the house. Suddenly, the real Sage Gautam appeared and found himself facing his lookalike. Indra panicked and tried to escape by transforming into a cat, but there was no way out. Gautam trembled in anger. He cursed Indra, turning him into a eunuch, and also turned Ahalya to stone. When Ahalya cried for forgiveness, Gautam felt compassion for her and said that her curse would end when Lord Rama came to the hermitage. Sad and shocked, he then left for the Himalayas."

Vishwamitra pointed to the stone lying inside the hut. That was Ahalya! Waiting and praying for Lord Rama to release her from this miserable existence. Vishwamitra requested Rama to touch the stone with his foot and release her from the curse. Rama obeyed his guru, not knowing what to expect. As soon as he touched the stone, it came alive and took the form of Ahalya. She cried with joy and thanked Rama for his mercy.

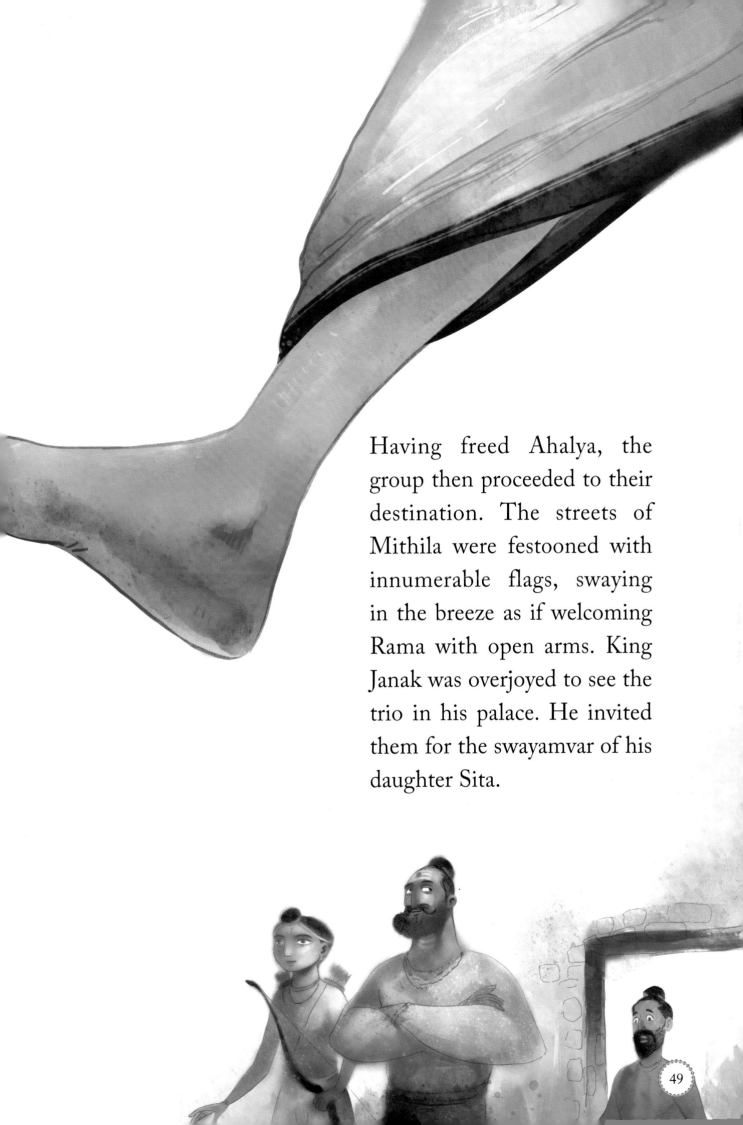

Having freed Ahalya, the group then proceeded to their destination. The streets of Mithila were festooned with innumerable flags, swaying in the breeze as if welcoming Rama with open arms. King Janak was overjoyed to see the trio in his palace. He invited them for the swayamvar of his daughter Sita.

She was to marry the one who was strong enough to break Shiva's bow. Rama and Laxman became alert at the very thought of the bow. It was the reason they had come to Mithila. Shiva's bow was gifted to him by Vishwakarma, the architect of the heavenly planets. He had made two such bows, one for Lord Shiva and the other for Lord Vishnu. Having used it once, Lord Shiva gifted it to King

Janak's ancestors. This is how the bow happened to be in his possession. The king then asked his soldiers to bring the bow to court. Five thousand strong men were needed to bring the bow on a cart that was pulled by 500 powerful bulls! Such was the weight of the bow. Just holding it must have given Mother Earth a chronic backache! The majestic bow filled the entire courtroom with awe. Was it a rainbow fallen from the sky or was it Mount Mandar used for churning the ocean? The courtroom was buzzing with excitement. But King Janak was not so excited. In fact, he was teary-eyed. No one had been able to break this bow to win the hand of his daughter. Some even thought he was a fool for having put up such a difficult condition, one that seemed impossible to fulfil. How would the darling daughter of the kingdom ever find a suitable husband with a crazy condition like this? But there was a reason behind it. When Sita was a child, her ball had rolled to where the bow was kept. She effortlessly pushed the bow to search for her ball. On finding it, she placed the bow back in its place. On another occasion, she had actually picked it up and ran to the garden, using it to pluck flowers.

The guards who saw this with their own eyes had fainted with shock. Thus, Janak had decided that the one who marries her should be her equal in strength, if not more. But now the king wondered if he had made a mistake, because he was yet to find such a person. Janak then asked Vishwamitra if Rama would like to try to lift the bow. Vishwamitra looked at the boy and gave him permission to do so. Rama stood up, walked to Vishwamitra for blessings and then turned to the bow. There was pin-drop silence in the courtroom. Would Rama succeed? Everyone waited with bated breath. Rama touched the bow, admired it, took grip of it and lifted it from the pedestal like an elephant effortlessly lifts a lotus. The entire assembly jumped up, roaring with relief and excitement.

But Rama was not done. He placed the bow vertically on the ground and strung it. And suddenly, everyone heard a boom. A sound so deafening that it was heard not just all the way in Ayodhya, but in every corner of the planet. The bow, the pride of Mithila, was broken from the centre. While Janak was speechless with joy, Rama simply stood there, as if he had done nothing extraordinary. Sita's friends ran to inform her that the bow had been broken and that it was time for her to see

her suitor. Sita entered the courtroom dressed in bridal clothes, holding a garland. But Rama was not ready for this. How could he get married in the absence of his dear father and mother?

And brothers! And the people of Ayodhya! Messengers were sent to Ayodhya to get Dasharatha's permission for the wedding and to invite him to Mithila. When the king heard the messengers, he was thrilled beyond imagination. The entire kingdom was invited to the wedding. The wedding procession was so huge that when Dasharatha, who was heading the procession, reached Mithila, the last person was still in Ayodhya. The procession was like a human sea stretching from Ayodhya to Mithila.

Meanwhile, Sage Vashishtha and Sage Vishwamitra were huddled together in another discussion. When they came back smiling, everyone was eager to know why. They addressed Janak and said, "We feel that since your daughter is being wedded to Rama, your second daughter Urmila can tie the knot with Laxman. And your brother's daughters can marry Bharat and Shatrughana. This way, our joy will multiply by four times." This was the best advice Janak had heard till now. Dasharatha too smiled and gave his approval. As the four weddings happened simultaneously, there was excitement in the air. The people of Mithila and Ayodhya had never experienced so much bliss before.

5

And the Winner is Manthara!

Dasharatha was running frantically, trying to escape the monster chasing him. He ran through the familiar streets of Ayodhya, looking for a place to hide. Why were the streets empty? The silence was deafening, interspersed with shrieks. Shrieks of the angry monster. He stopped to knock at his minister's door, but suddenly a hand gripped his shoulder. He struggled to free himself. He flung his arms…and the moment he hit him there was a crashing sound!

Dasharatha was jolted back to reality. He was not on the streets, but in his royal bed. It was a dream! Unable to go back to sleep, he climbed out of his bed and paced across the room. A glance at the life-sized oval mirror revealed white hair close to his ears, as if whispering to him. You are too old now. Step down from the throne.

Yes, he thought. It was time to put an end to these nightmares. In the morning, he convened a special meeting of all those who mattered to him. His ministers, advisers, gurus and family. Those who loved him unconditionally and whom he loved in return. Once everyone arrived, he announced his decision. He was stepping down from the throne. And he wanted to appoint Rama as his heir. Was this acceptable to everyone?

"Long live King Dasharatha!" boomed the entire courtroom, the people expressing their approval and joy. "We cannot think of anyone better than Rama to rule Ayodhya!"

Dasharatha felt a burden lift off his shoulders. Though he had their wholehearted support, he felt a lingering trace of fear in his heart. He even knew the source of that fear… but he didn't want to think about that now. He had to coronate Rama immediately, the very next day. All of Ayodhya erupted in celebration. Everyone loved Rama. He made them happy with his caring nature, his wisdom, his courage and the various noble traits that he possessed.

Sumanthara, Dasharatha's right hand, had kicked off preparations for the coronation with the help of Sage Vashishtha. Meanwhile, Dasharatha went to meet Rama, his life and soul. Twenty-five years had passed gazing at his precious gem. But it was never enough. Rama had an enchanting effect on everyone. He stole everyone's love and attention with his generosity and virtues.

Dasharatha embraced Rama tightly and informed him about the unanimous decision of coronating him as king of Ayodhya. Rama noticed that although his father was excited, there was also a streak of anxiety on his face. What was he hiding? Dasharatha revealed his fears; the nightmares he had been seeing the last few days and also the ill omen that meant he would either meet with an accident or death.

Hence, the emergency coronation. The ceremony would happen even though Bharat was away at his maternal home.

Meanwhile, destiny was turning its wheels. Manthara, Keikeyi's maid, had never liked Rama. When she learnt of his coronation scheduled for the very next day, her heart skipped a beat. Her scheming mind wasted no time in plotting wicked plans to stop it. She scurried to Keikeyi's room to break the bad news. But to her horror, Keikeyi thought it was wonderful news. She even rewarded Manthara with an expensive necklace for being the bearer of such auspicious news. Manthara was flabbergasted. "Are you mad?" she screamed at Keikeyi. "Once he becomes king, his mother Kaushalya will be all-powerful and your position will be that of their servant. Is that what you want?" Keikeyi was not convinced, but she chose to remain silent. Encouraged by her silence, Manthara continued to spew poison, "Not just you, even your son Bharat will be a servant of Rama and Kaushalya. At least think about his future."

Keikeyi loved Rama like her own son, but Manthara's wicked thoughts began to impact her and soon she was agreeing with everything the evil woman had to say. "What should I do now, Manthara?" she asked for advice. Manthara was ready with the solution. "Remember the two boons the king gave you many years ago? It's time to encash them now!" she declared in a sinister tone. Keikeyi was impressed with Manthara's memory. She herself had forgotten about the boons.

Thousands of years ago, Dasharatha was in a battle, fighting on behalf of the demigods. He had nearly lost his life, when his bold and beautiful charioteer Keikeyi saved the day for him. Displaying tremendous courage, she stuck her finger in the chariot wheel to ensure that it does not fall off, giving Dasharatha enough time to vanquish his enemy. Grateful for what she had done, Dasharatha offered her two boons. Keikeyi saved those boons for the future, because she did not need anything apart from what she already had.

"You will remind Dasharatha of the two boons and here is what you will demand. Your first boon will be that Bharat should be crowned the new king. And your second wish will be that Rama should leave the kingdom and go to the forest for 14 years."

Manthara's eyes gleamed with delight. All was going as per plan. Keikeyi was under her control, willing to obey her orders. That night when Dasharatha came to her palace, she asked for the boons, as instructed by Manthara.

Dasharatha fell to the floor, writhing in pain. He begged her to change her mind. He was willing to make Bharat the king, but why sentence Rama to exile? Separated from his beloved Rama, he would surely die! But Keikeyi had become so hard-hearted that even the thought of her husband's death did not move her. She remained adamant. He was duty-bound to give her the two boons. After a night of pleading and begging, Dasharatha had no option but to call Rama for a meeting.

He was in no condition to speak, so Keikeyi asked Rama to leave the palace immediately. Rama was neither happy when he was given the throne, nor unhappy when it was taken away from him. He looked at this as an opportunity to live with sages in the forest and gain spiritual insight.

However, Laxman and Sita would not let him leave alone. Both of them demanded to accompany him. As Rama, Sita and Laxman prepared to leave for the forest, the entire kingdom of Ayodhya plunged into darkness. Life without Rama was unbearable. They too decided to leave with him. Not a single soul wanted to remain in Ayodhya. Bharat could be the king of a ghost kingdom.

Rama bade farewell to his mother, father, friends and well-wishers and climbed into the chariot that would drop him to the outskirts of the kingdom. Following him was all of Ayodhya. Dasharatha ran after his son to stop him, but his weak legs could not carry him far and he fell down in grief. His worst fears had come true! His Rama was leaving him again.

6

Laxman's Vow

Was there anyone who could stop Rama from leaving Ayodhya? In this gloomy hour, the sun too had disappeared behind the mountains, unable to tolerate the pain of Rama's departure.

At sunset, Rama halted for the night on the banks of River Tamas. The citizens of Ayodhya occupied the entire bank such that the river of humans paralleled the river of water.

After the fateful day, Rama opened up to Laxman, sharing his feelings, "Laxman, my brother! I'm glad you are with me. I'm much more confident with you around. I hope mother and father stop crying. I'm sure Bharat will take care of them." Overcome with fatigue, he drifted off to sleep. Only two people resisted sleep, Laxman and Sumanthara, who was going to chariot them to the forest. The duo sat under a tree, unloading their hearts.

It had been an emotional day for Laxman. Especially when he went to bid farewell to his mother Sumitra. Would she stop him from leaving?

He shuddered… what if she breaks down and doesn't stop crying? He decided he would simply inform her and run out without giving her a chance to respond. But he was so wrong! He had badly misjudged his mother—like all children do! Her response had taken him by surprise. Even before he could speak, she said, "Laxman, you are born to serve Rama. From now on, Rama is like your father and Sita is like your mother. May you be happy serving them." Only then did she break down. Laxman hugged her, understanding her grief. Fortunately for Laxman, his wife Urmila also supported his decision of going with Rama.

Immersed in thoughts, he was startled to hear a smooth, silvery voice speaking to him. "O hero! I am Nidradevi, the goddess of sleep. Let me serve you. You are exhausted and need rejuvenation."

Laxman not only refused her proposal, he also put his hands up in the air and took a vow, "I vow that for the next 14 years I will not sleep a wink, day or night!" Nidradevi was aghast. "How can you not sleep? It's against the law of nature," she protested. Laxman suggested, "Please go to my wife Urmila in Ayodhya. She will accept your service on my behalf."

When Nidradevi reached Ayodhya, Urmila accepted her offer and slept for the next 14 years, during the day on behalf of Laxman and at night for herself.

After Nidradevi left, Laxman heard footsteps approaching him. As the figure came closer, he could see it was Rama. What was it that he wanted to say in the middle of the night? He hurried towards him. "Laxman, I was looking for you. It is not right to inconvenience the citizens of Ayodhya."

"Let us leave now so that they have no option but to go back to Ayodhya." Rama was right. The Ayodhyawasis were so determined, they would follow the trio wherever they went. Laxman gave his approval and the three of them crossed the river in the quiet of the night. They were accompanied by Sumanthara, who would return after dropping them at the edge of the forest.

After many hours of travel, they rested under a huge fig tree. No sooner had they stretched their legs than they found themselves surrounded by a horde of tribals with beating drums and fire torches. Anticipating an attack, Laxman readied himself with his bow. However, the chief stepped forward and said with folded hands, "Welcome to Sringaberpur."

"Guha? The king of the Nishada tribe! A friend of our father!" Rama exclaimed, smiling broadly, and rushed to embrace him. The chief was dressed in leather garments and shoes, an embroidered waist-belt embedded with tiger nails, armlets and anklets made of stones, a necklace of colourful shells on his chest and, a multicoloured helmet decorated with various feathers! He looked like an interesting person.

Happy to see the famous prince, he offered to be at Rama's service. Guha had already heard about Rama leaving Ayodhya. He said, "I am a humble servant of your father and your divine self."

"Whatever I own, thousands of boats, this kingdom, it is all at your disposal. Please stay here and allow us to serve you." Rama assured Guha that he would not need his hospitality. He preferred to sleep under the tree and eat fruits and herbs. Soon, Rama and Sita were fast asleep on a velvety green bed of grass that Laxman had lovingly prepared for them.

Morning came and the trio decided to continue their journey by boat. Once Sita was comfortably seated in the boat, Rama put his foot inside. Guha and Sumanthara wanted to follow him, but Rama would not hear of it. He assured Guha that he would be back after 14 years, on his way to Ayodhya. And he requested Sumanthara to do everything possible for the well-being of his father and the Ikshvaku dynasty.

The boat departed, leaving behind many heavy hearts. It was not easy for anyone, but Rama did what he had to do. Life would not be easy for any of them, and yet, it would go on.

Sorrow and Hope

"Kaushalya, how could I be foolish enough to send Rama, whom I love more than life, to the forest? How I wish I had not listened to Keikeyi!" lamented Dasharatha, who was slowly dying from the pain of separation. Absorbed in remembering Rama, Dasharatha left his body like a yogi in trance. None of King Dasharatha's sons was present in Ayodhya. Messengers were sent to call Bharat and Shatrughana back from the kingdom of Kekeya.

Vashishtha had instructed the messengers not to reveal the facts to the princes—the depressing facts of Rama's exile and Dasharatha's death. But judging by their cryptic message about returning urgently and their forlorn faces, Bharat knew something was seriously wrong. Moreover, he had had a nightmare about his father falling into a deep pit and a demoness dragging him away on a chariot. The dream was so ominous that it had rattled Bharat. To him it meant the funeral fire of either his father, brother Laxman or himself. The two brothers left with the messengers without any delay. It took them eight days to reach Ayodhya. But this wasn't Ayodhya, was it? The city was creepily silent.

Crows and jackals were crying. "Where are we?" Bharat asked the chariot driver. "Why does it look like a ghost town? Even the trees appear sad." Unable to find his father in his palace, he rushed to his mother's palace. Seeing Keikeyi in a blissful condition was a complete contrast to the environment outside. Bharat was totally confused. "What has happened in Ayodhya? Where is my father? Why is everyone sad? Call my father right now. I want his blessings." Bharat was unable to control the dam of his emotions. "Your father is dead," announced Keikeyi without any trace of sorrow. Her words struck Bharat like lightning and he lost his balance and collapsed.

Her casual utterance of this tragedy had only added to his shock. She continued, "Everyone has to die one day. Why cry about something that cannot be stopped?" With tears flowing down his cheeks, he said "I thought father had planned to surprise me by calling me for Rama's coronation. But he shocked me by leaving me forever. What were his last words?" "His last words were—O Rama, Laxman, Sita, those who see you return will be most fortunate." Keikeyi explained how the three of them had left for the forest so that Bharat could become king. Shock and disbelief engulfed him! His mother was responsible for all the terrible things happening. "My dear son, I did this for you. You can become the king now!" she explained.

Bharat let out a loud roar. A volcano of grief poured out from him. He folded his hands and prayed to Lord Rama for forgiveness. "What happiness will I feel by being the cause of my father's death and the cause of my beloved brother's exile? I died as soon as I heard this news. A dead body cannot be happy. Nor can it rule a kingdom. Why did you do this to me?" he shouted at Keikeyi for having caused him endless grief. "I will make sure that none of your wicked desires are fulfilled. I will throw you out of Ayodhya." Keikeyi's plans had backfired on her. "Rama deserves to be the king of Ayodhya. I will make this happen, come what may! I will not be a party to your sins by accepting the crown of Ayodhya," Bharat vowed.

King Dasharatha's funeral and the 12 days of mourning went by in a blur. There wasn't a moment for Bharat to reflect or nurse his wounds. Soon, it was time to attend court and come to terms with reality. Bharat and Shatrughana entered the courtroom together, after weeks of mourning. Sage Vashishtha said, "O noble prince, it is now your duty to fulfil your father's words. Dasharatha has awarded the kingdom to you. Please accept the throne."

Vashishtha's words felt like stones that were hitting the dam of his emotions and tearing it down. Tears flowed like a waterfall. He gathered his strength so that he could explain that he would not be sitting on a throne. "Just like a body is useless without the presence of life, I am useless without the presence of Rama. I refuse to sit on the throne tainted by the blood of my father. The king of Ayodhya is Rama and I will ensure he comes back." A smile flickered on the anxious faces in front of him. Sage Vashishtha was in tears, proud of his disciple.

"We will go to the forest and bring Rama back." A loud cheer erupted as soon as Bharat said these words. Any plan to bring Rama back was the best plan.

The first phase was put into action. A road was built from Ayodhya to the forest. Potters, sculptors, weavers, tailors, ministers, all marched on this journey.

Oblivious to Bharat's army marching to meet him, Rama was enjoying a moment of quiet in his newly constructed hut. Laxman had taken great pains to make this abode for Rama. It was so spectacular that Rama and Sita could not look away. Especially the canopy above their bed, made of leaves and peacock feathers. The happiness on their faces made all the effort worthwhile.

Suddenly, their peace was interrupted by loud noises. Laxman climbed a sal tree to see what the commotion was about. He climbed down visibly shaken. "It's Bharat with an army; he now wants to kill you!" he declared angrily. If only Laxman could hear Bharat saying, "We will not leave without Rama. How lucky these birds and animals are who reside here with him."

The minute he reached, Bharat ran inside the hut and fell at Rama's feet. Rama picked up his brother and embraced him fondly. Just his embrace was enough to make Bharat and Shatrughana feel rejuvenated. Rama placed their heads on his lap and caressed them with his tender hands. "Where is our father?" he asked suddenly. Bharat could not meet his eyes. He replied, "Father died a sad man, remembering you. Since all of this has happened because of me, the only way for you to forgive me is by coming back to Ayodhya. We have come all the way to take you home."

Tears gushed out of Rama's eyes remembering his dear father. He swooned and collapsed on the ground with a thud. Sita ran to him and sprinkled some water on his face. He opened his eyes slowly and whispered, "I have no reason to return now. But do not blame yourself or mother Keikeyi. It was my destiny."

"But I am not capable of ruling the kingdom. A donkey cannot compete with a horse. The kingdom needs your principled guidance," Bharat argued and pleaded, but Rama did not relent.

In order to break this deadlock, Bharat offered a solution. "If I sit on the throne, I will feel that I have cheated you. This dilemma can be solved only if I install your footwear on the throne. The footwear will assure me that I am ruling the kingdom on your behalf." Rama did not object to this proposal. Bharat took a solemn vow, "I vow that for the next 14 years, I shall dress in bark and skin, eat only roots and fruits and live outside the city of Ayodhya. And if I do not see you on the day when these painful 14 years end, I will jump into a pyre and end my life."

Rama embraced Bharat to his heart's content, promising that he would surely come back on time. He also pulled Shatrughana into his loving embrace and patted his brothers' heads.

Bharat held Rama's slippers on his head and began the journey back to Ayodhya. Next day, along with Shatrughana, he left the city of Ayodhya to reside in a village known as Nandigram. In his small hut, he made a throne on which he kept Rama's footwear. For the next 14 years, Bharat lived in that hut and ran the kingdom of Ayodhya on behalf of Rama.

Demon or Angel?

Sita had woken up to a bright sunny morning with a song in her heart. Of all the things in the forest, her greatest joy was the sight of beautiful flowers in every colour. Wherever she looked, pretty flowers smiled at her. Today, she thought, was a good day to make a flower garland for Rama. With a basket in hand, she began plucking flowers from bushes and trees.

Out of the blue, she felt her feet being lifted off the ground. Holding her from the waist, someone was lifting her up in the sky. The basket fell from her hand and the falling flowers created a mini-rainbow in mid-air. With her feet dangling down and her hands up in the sky, she cried for help. Almost simultaneously, she heard a shriek from Laxman. Rama had nearly fainted upon seeing Sita's plight.

A mammoth monster three times bigger than the tallest tree of the jungle had captured the delicate Sita. In his hand was a spear skewering dead lions, tigers, deer, wolves and elephant heads. He wore a serpent around his waist as a belt, preventing the elephant skin from falling off his body.

The demon could not scare the brothers though. They quickly attacked him with arrows. But their arrows only bounced off his body. He laughed when he saw the shocked faces of Rama and Laxman.

In a thunderous voice he boasted, "My name is Viradha and I have the blessings of Brahma's boons—the strength of twenty-five thousand elephants and the power to face any weapon. You tiny humans are no match for me. Go away and leave this lady for me." Joyously, he picked up his spear, spinning it like he would spin a drumstick. And without a warning, he hurled it at Rama. Rama, alert as ever, broke the spear with his arrow. But he could not do anything more than that. His arrows were not affecting the demon. Not even a scratch.

The brothers changed their strategy. They ran towards the demon. By now, he had put Sita down to use both his hands to fight his enemies. When they came closer, he grabbed them with both his hands. What fools they were to run into his grip! But Rama and Laxman used all their might to cut his arms with their sword. The demon fell, crushing many trees on the ground. But he still did not give up. He turned and twisted his body, trying to crush the brothers with his weight. Rama them put his foot on Viradha to prevent him from moving. The demon slowly stopped struggling and became motionless. Rama told Laxman to dig a pit to bury him.

A palpable change was now overcoming Viradha. His face was calm and serene. No anger, no envy, no cruelty. Eyes shut, he was chanting in yogic meditation. When he opened his eyes again, he said in a soft voice, "My Lord, I am grateful to you for liberating me from this body. In my last birth I was Tumburu, a gandharva and a celestial being. Since I was extremely beautiful and talented, the wealthiest of all demigods, Kubera had appointed me as his personal assistant. Becoming proud of my achievements, I started neglecting my duties.

In a fit of anger, Kubera cursed me to live like a demon who has no duties and no discipline. I could return to him the day you came and freed me from this miserable body. Now, please bury me and free me." Fascinated by the demon's story, Rama and Laxman pushed him inside the pit. No sooner had they covered the pit than a very handsome form emerged from it. It was Tumburu himself in his original gandharva form. His smile filled the whole forest with divine music. He folded his hands in gratitude and vanished in thin air.

9

The Foolish Surpanakha

"What a beautiful day it is today." Surpanakha was enjoying flying in the forests of Panchavati. She had decided that it was a good day to find a handsome boy to marry. Her brother Ravana had killed her husband. "Perhaps he came between Ravana and his sword by mistake. Yes, it must have been an accident," she thought out loud. She did not want to believe that her brother had killed her husband. "Ravana gifted me a kingdom after all, didn't he? Wait! Who's that?"

She had caught a glimpse of someone who looked too handsome to be true. He was unbelievable. "This is the one I was waiting for, my dream boy!" She was in a frenzy now, looking at his lotus-like eyes, teeth like the moon and hair as black as clouds. She flew down and hid behind a tree to get a better look at him. "Oh, he looks like a god!" she exclaimed, swooning with infatuation.

With great hope and anticipation, she walked towards Rama's hut. In her opinion, she was a perfect match for him. She imagined that her bent back, steely red hair and sunken eyes complemented his black hair, bright eyes and supple body. She couldn't wait to know who he was, and asked right away, "Who are you? Tell me frankly, why you are here?"

"I am Rama, the son of Dasharatha." Rama couldn't help but smile at the sight of this demoness, as he could see right through her deception. Nonetheless, he enquired, "Who are you, beautiful lady?"

Swooning at his velvety voice, Surpanakha boasted about herself, "You must have heard of me, Surpanakha, famous for my sharp blade-like nails and shape-shifting abilities. My name creates terror! You must have surely heard of the demon-king Ravana, my brother. And Kumbhakaran. My third brother Vibhishan is a rebel, the black sheep of my family. Now, I want to admit that I have given my heart to you. If you marry me, we will freely dwell in this forest inaccessible to humans. Look at me, I am perfect for you."

Rama chuckled at her foolish proposal. The more he laughed, the more lovable she found him to be. Rama then burst her bubble of love. Pointing to Sita, he said, "You will not be able to live with my wife Sita. I suggest you marry my brother Laxman."

When she looked at Laxman, he was equally handsome. Not a bad idea! She hopped towards him and repeated her proposal to him. He also refused, saying he was a servant of Rama and not fit for a regal beauty like her. Agreeing with his logic, she hopped back to Rama.

But Rama had gone inside the hut with Sita. Seeing him in close proximity to his wife, Surpanakha boiled with anger. How dare that witch snatch him away from her? She shrieked at Rama, "This puny woman will not let you marry me? I will kill her right now. Then we can be happy together." She lunged at Sita, intending to attack with her sharp nails. Rama immediately signalled to Laxman, gesturing how to tackle her. He darted toward Surpanakha, grabbing her hair with one hand. Using his other hand and a dagger he carried in his waist-belt, Laxman slashed her nose in one swift motion. The wicked demoness howled in pain, with blood gushing out her nose. She grabbed him with both hands, wanting to fly away with Laxman captive. But he wielded his dagger again and chopped off both her ears this time.

Surpanakha stamped her feet, rolled on the ground and tried to hit back at Laxman. But she felt too weak to stay any further and ran into the forest screaming for revenge. She had to go tell Ravana everything. He would surely act on her behalf.

When Ravana saw his sister he hardly recognised her. She could barely talk straight. She got so caught up in describing Rama and Laxman's beauty that she forgot the rest of the story. Coming to the point, she said, "Rama and Laxman are just harmless boys. Fragile and weak, incapable of competing with you. But it's because of Sita that they dared to attack your sister. They are so obsessed with her that they will defeat you too." Ravana was now confused. Surpanakha was constantly contradicting herself. She continued blabbering, "Sita is so beautiful, there is no one like her in all of Lanka. If you love me, dear Ravana, get me the bodies of the two brothers and that cunning lady, Sita. I want to be the one to kill her. Please satisfy my hunger and thirst, my brother," she pleaded.

Ravana was sufficiently
instigated to send his goons
to bring the three culprits to
him. "Two heads and a lady, that's what
I want," he thundered, much to
the joy of Surpanakha, who
clapped in glee.

10

The Fatal Chase

Sita was milking a tigress today (after the cubs had had their share, of course). Later, guided by the bears, she would find the most succulent fruits and berries without any difficulties. She had even begun to understand insect talk. Almost! After 13 years, Sita had become an erudite resident of the forest.

After her encounter with Viradha, she had become more alert. While plucking a bunch of flowers, she caught some movement behind the bushes. What she saw was dazzling. Frolicking around the trees was an enchanting animal. It was a deer... Or was it? It was nothing like any deer she had seen before. Golden in colour with silver spots. Its white stomach studded with blue diamonds.

Sita fell in love with this fascinating creature. Dropping everything, she ran to the hut, eager to tell Rama about it. "You won't believe it, but I saw the most beautiful animal ever. I want that animal with me!" Rama and Laxman went outside to see what Sita was gushing about. On spotting the deer, Laxman understood at once who it was. "It is not a deer. Not one of the other deer is associating with him. It must be Maricha, the shape-shifting demon."

Sita interrupted him, "The deer has stolen my heart. My dear Rama, please bring me this deer. I want to take it back to Ayodhya with me," she pleaded.

Rama readied himself to leave and fulfil Sita's desire. When Laxman tried to stop him, he said, "Even if it is a demon, I must go and destroy it. Moreover, in the last 25 years, Sita has never asked me for anything."

"This is the first time that she has expressed a desire. So, I must try to fulfil it. You stay here and guard her. Make sure she is protected. Keep your bow and arrow ready."

With a bow in his hand and a sword tucked in his waist, Rama began the chase. He noticed that the deer was behaving peculiarly. It kept turning around to make sure Rama was following it. Sometimes, it would disappear from one spot and magically appear at another spot. By now, he was sure that this was a demon taking him away from Laxman and Sita. Without wasting more time, he drew an arrow and took aim. The wounded deer hit the ground. But lying in a pool of blood was not the deer, but a demon. It was Maricha, in his original rakshasa form. Just before dying, he called out, "Hey Sita! Hey Laxman!" imitating the voice of Rama.

The entire forest echoed with that call. Rama was shocked. The demon had cleverly planned to separate Laxman from Sita too.

She heard Rama's distress call and cried out, "Laxman, did you hear that? Did you hear Rama calling for help? Run. Go and help him. He's in danger!" Sita was in a state of panic. She had never heard her husband cry out for help. But Laxman seemed unconcerned. "Why are you not going?" she hysterically screamed.

As much as Laxman tried to calm her down by saying that this was not Rama's voice, Sita would not hear any of it. She cried, she argued, she even hurt Laxman's feelings to force him to go into the forest to help Rama.

Laxman left. A sadhu (an ascetic) dressed in saffron robes, was just waiting for this. He immediately appeared at Sita's door to beg for alms, chanting Vedic hymns to catch Sita's attention, who was sobbing inside. His plan had worked perfectly. Maricha had done his job well. Ravana was thankful to his sister Surpanakha for describing the beauty of Sita and urging him to kidnap her. He would have given half his kingdom to have her.

Sita thought that there was something fishy about the sadhu, nonetheless, she came out to give him some fruits. Ravana immediately transformed to reveal his real, demonic form and grabbed her hand. He lifted her and carried her out of the cottage. Sita screamed at the top of her lungs, hoping that her husband would hear her. Her chilling scream scared all the birds in the vicinity, but help was nowhere around. Ravana's magical aerial chariot, known as Pushpak Viman, came down and he stepped inside, taking her to an unknown destination.

From the chariot she could see animals, birds and trees, all looking at her. She prayed for their help, but how could they help her? She regretted her desire to have the golden deer. Never had she been separated from Rama before. Suddenly, she saw hope. It was Jatayu, the vulture. A family friend. He would surely help her. And she was right. Jatayu heard Sita telling him to convey her message to Rama, that she had been abducted by Ravana. But he could not simply watch Ravana take Sita away forcibly. He was old but not a coward. He would fight Ravana and save Sita even if he died in the process. The gigantic bird gathered all his strength and attacked the plane.

The plane lost its balance due to the mini
tornado created by Jatayu's flapping wings.
The size of the bird filled Ravana with fear.
One wing was enough to hold a chariot. His
long beak and sharp claws looked brutal. But
Ravana was not chicken-hearted. He was shrewd and wicked.
He saw that the bird was really old. Nothing to fear!

With one swoop of his wing, Jatayu dislodged Ravana's crown
and attacked the Pushpak Viman. He even warned the demon
to let go of Sita but it fell on deaf ears. Ravana was too powerful.
Every time Jatayu ripped off his arms, they would regenerate.
Try what he may, the old bird was not able to defeat the demon
king. Ravana attacked his wings, which were his weakest parts
and with one clean swipe, a wing was damaged beyond repair.
Jatayu lost his balance and plummeted to the ground,
leaving Ravana free to continue on his journey.

Meanwhile, Rama and Laxman had returned to their cottage only to find Sita missing. Rama called out for Sita as loudly as he could. He began running around searching for her. Finally, he cupped his face in his hands and cried, "She's gone! She's gone!"

He said, "Laxman, without Sita I will die. I cannot return to Ayodhya without her. How will I face everyone? I have lost everything, including my kingdom, my father and Sita."

Laxman tried to console his grieving brother. Together they set out to search for Sita. Some clues, some telltale signs of what could have happened. They found Jatayu waiting for their arrival. He was half-dead and had managed to stay alive only so that he could fulfil his duty of conveying Sita's message. Both Rama and Laxman were filled with sadness when they heard the story from him and they were sadder still when Jatayu's soul left his body in Rama's lap. But for the bird, dying in Rama's lap was his ticket to liberation.

Wandering here and there looking for Sita, they reached Pampa Sarovar, which housed Matanga Rishi's ashram at the foothills of Rishimukha mountain. They were welcomed by Shabari, a frail and old woman of short stature and sunken cheeks. However, her aura suggested that she was no ordinary human being. She sat down, reverentially offering them a plate full of berries, the best that she had gathered from the forest. Rama found them so tasty that he could not stop eating. Never before had berries tasted better. Shabari must have taken such pains to gather them. She revealed, "My guru Matanga Rishi told me that you would come. I have waited 13 years for you. For 13 years I have been expecting you to come any day, any time. Each day I have washed the hermitage for you. Fetched fresh water, made a garland of fresh flowers and collected berries for you. The only reason I kept waiting was my guru's instruction. "You wait here. Rama will come. You serve him and then come back to me."

Next, she took a palm leaf and began to scribble on the leaf using a peacock-feather quill dipped in some sort of organic ink. The brothers curiously looked on. "This is the map of the Kishikandha region. Just follow this trail and you will soon spot the wonder monkeys. Their leader is the one who can actually help you find Sita."

"Now, please allow me to go back to my guru."

When Rama nodded his head, she invoked a yogic fire within her body and burnt down her external form. A brilliant flash lit the entire forest.

The brothers left the ashram, following the path Shabari had suggested. All that they carried with them from the ashram were memories, tears and hope of finding Sita. While Laxman was lost in his own thoughts, Rama walked ahead. Suddenly, he froze!

11

The Invisible Bond

"Does this make any sense, Laxman?" said Rama pointing in one direction. Laxman followed his finger and saw a fragile-looking short old sanyasi with a begging pot in one hand and a stick in the other.

Rama was right. It did not make any sense. A mendicant sanyasi begging in a jungle where no humans lived? Could he be a demon in disguise? The begging sanyasi also saw them. At that very moment, his body began to quiver and tremble. Rivers of tears were flowing from his eyes. He felt every bone in his body melting. It took him a minute to get a hold of himself. Embarrassed, he walked towards Rama and Laxman.

It was the first time Hanuman was meeting Rama. Disguised as a sanyasi, he had come to verify who these strangers were. Were they any danger to his master Sugreeva, the wonder monkey? He had no idea why he was feeling such joy on seeing them. Not only him, the animals also shared this euphoria. They constantly nuzzled the duo with great affection. Not just wild animals, even trees bent to offer their salutations. These were surely not ordinary people.

Hanuman bent his head in respect and enquired, "You look like kings but are dressed like sages, complete misfits in the forest. What is the purpose of your visit?"

He was greeted with complete silence. They only stared at him, penetrating his soul. "If you are genuinely a beggar, then what is a diamond necklace doing around your neck? You are too strange to be a beggar!" Rama said upon closely observing the sanyasi. Hanuman felt the ground slipping below his feet. "I don't believe this. Can you see my necklace?" he enquired in awe.

Rama couldn't understand why this sanyasi was so bewildered. He looked at Laxman and shrugged. But Laxman was equally bewildered. He said, "I don't see any necklace!"

Hanuman dropped to his knees and folded his hands in reverence. "My mother was right. She said my master would come looking for me. And the one who can see my invisible necklace is my master!"

What stood in front of them now was not an old sanyasi but a well-built wonder monkey. He touched Rama's feet with his bulky hands and placed his head on his lord's feet, wetting them with tears.

Rama and Laxman smiled when he said, "I am Hanuman, the servant of Sugreeva." After finishing his education with the sun god, Hanuman had offered to give guru dakshina. The sun god had asked for a very unusual fee. He wanted Hanuman to serve his son Sugreeva, a wonder monkey, and protect him from his own brother Vali. And that is what Hanuman had done selflessly.

Just by looking at Hanuman, Rama was convinced that he and Sugreeva could help them find Sita. Laxman stepped forward and said, "O Hanuman, we have been looking for you. I am Laxman, Rama's younger brother and son of Dasharatha…" And Laxman continued to narrate their tale of tragedy, starting from exile to the kidnapping of Sita. "And we are here, on the advice of Shabari, to meet the king of wonder monkeys, who can help us find Sita."

Hanuman's face lit up with great joy and he exclaimed, "Please allow me the fortune of carrying the two of you on my back to meet Sugreeva, who lives on top of the Rishimukha mountain."

Soon both the brothers, seated on Hanuman's broad shoulders, were cruising up the lofty mountain.

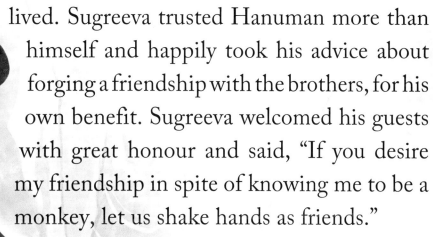

He carried them to the entrance of the cave where Sugreeva lived. Sugreeva trusted Hanuman more than himself and happily took his advice about forging a friendship with the brothers, for his own benefit. Sugreeva welcomed his guests with great honour and said, "If you desire my friendship in spite of knowing me to be a monkey, let us shake hands as friends."

Rama not only grabbed Sugreeva's hand but pulled him in a tight embrace. Sugreeva was overwhelmed to receive so much love from a stranger.

All he could see was pure, compassionate love. The two new-found friends stared at each other for a really long time. Sugreeva began expressing his life's complexities to Rama in great detail. Rama patiently heard him out. As he spoke about the traumatic life he was leading, Sugreeva broke down and begged Rama to help him now that they were friends.

"I, the son of Dasharatha, descendant of the glorious Ikshvaku dynasty, take a vow that I will annihilate your enemy very soon," Rama declared with great anger and determination in his eyes.

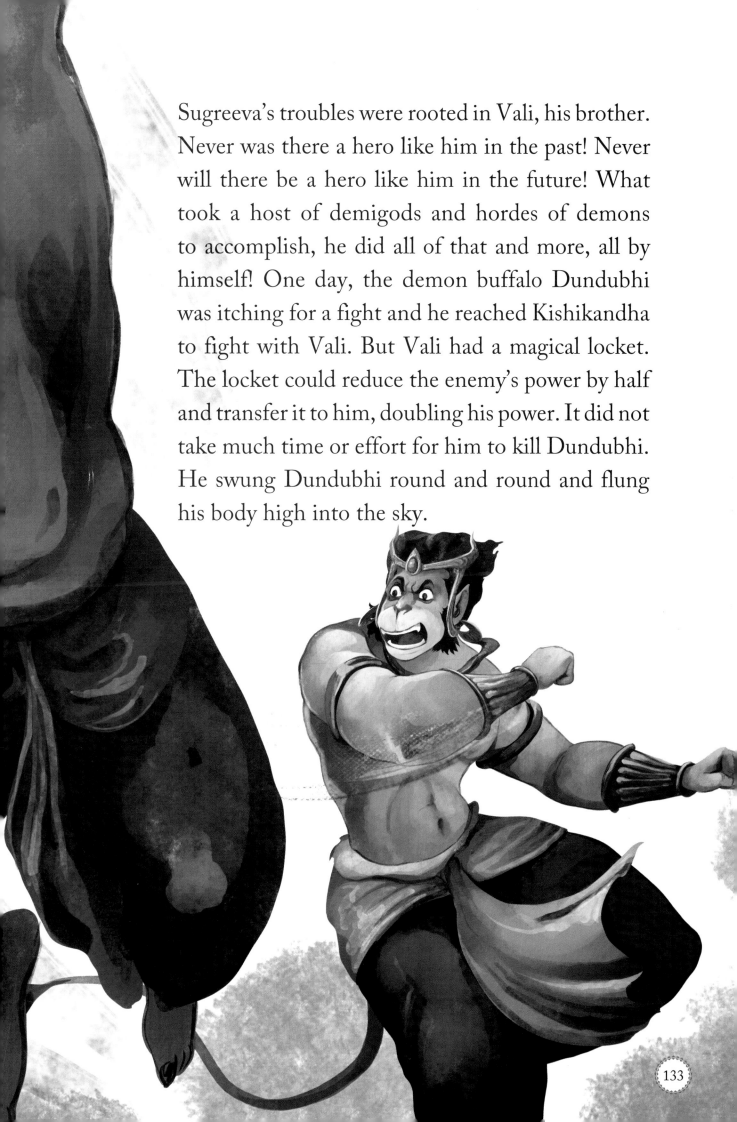

Sugreeva's troubles were rooted in Vali, his brother. Never was there a hero like him in the past! Never will there be a hero like him in the future! What took a host of demigods and hordes of demons to accomplish, he did all of that and more, all by himself! One day, the demon buffalo Dundubhi was itching for a fight and he reached Kishikandha to fight with Vali. But Vali had a magical locket. The locket could reduce the enemy's power by half and transfer it to him, doubling his power. It did not take much time or effort for him to kill Dundubhi. He swung Dundubhi round and round and flung his body high into the sky.

The humungous body fell on Rishimukha mountain, the abode of holy saints. The impact of the fall splattered blood and flesh in all directions. It not only polluted the ashram of Matanga Rishi, but also drenched him in blood. Who dared to throw a demon in his ashram? Which fool dared to play with fire? From his divine vision, he knew it was Vali. "The head of the evil-doer will split into a thousand pieces if he dares to enter the sacred Rishimukha mountain," he pronounced.

But the story did not end here. Dundubhi's brother, Mayavi turned up the next day to avenge his brother's death. Vali accepted his challenge and ran to catch him. Sugreeva joined the chase just in case his brother needed help. Soon, Mayavi disappeared into an underground cave. Vali also entered the cave. But before entering, he instructed Sugreeva to wait for him at the entrance. If he did not return in one month, Sugreeva should consider him dead and go back to the kingdom. Days turned into weeks and weeks turned into months. For an entire year, Sugreeva waited outside the cave. Finally, assuming Vali to be dead, he sealed the opening of the cave with rocks and went back and took over the kingdom. He had not even settled down when Vali appeared. He kicked Sugreeva in anger and accused him of usurping his kingdom. Fearing for his life, Sugreeva ran, leaving behind his wife and family.

He ran all over the world trying to save his skin, but the only safe place he found was the Rishimukha mountain, which was out of bounds for the mighty Vali. Since then, he had been living on the mountain, hiding from his brother and burning in the fire of revenge.

Sugreeva now made a proposal. If Rama could help him kill Vali, Sugreeva would reciprocate and help Rama find his wife Sita. The two friends vowed to help each other.

12

Brothers at War

"VAAAAAAAAALLLLLLLLLLLIIIIIIIIIIIIIII!" The pain in his heart came out as a shriek so loud that it surprised Sugreeva himself. It shattered the quietude of Kishikandha. Sugreeva was following Rama's instructions to the hilt. He had been reluctant to challenge Vali but Rama assured him by saying, "You will fight, but I will kill."

Tightening his waist cloth, Sugreeva yelled out yet again, openly challenging his elder brother. He looked behind to confirm that Rama was present to back him up. Rama, Laxman and Hanuman had positioned themselves behind a tree. Rama nodded in encouragement.

The sight of Sugreeva triggered a volcano of hatred in Vali. He smacked his arms with his palms. The resulting sound was so thunderous that it caused nearby rocks to crack. Vali's wife tried to intervene but there was no stopping him.

The two hulks stood facing each other with eyes full of hatred. It was a do-or-die battle. Leaping high in the air, Vali pounced on his brother. His fist landed on Sugreeva's head with such power that blood spurted out in all directions. Sugreeva rolled on the ground in pain. Quickly pulling himself up, he uprooted an entire tree. He whacked his brother so hard that Vali reeled in pain. Sugreeva laughed loudly like a mad man, whacking Vali with all his strength. Vali recovered and punched Sugreeva's elbow, causing the tree to fall from his hand. Now both were weaponless and battered.

Next, the brothers struck each other's chests. Sparks flew out from their iron-like chests and the sound of the collision resounded till the end of the universe.

Even the gods had assembled to watch this gruesome fight. The number of cuts, bruises and wounds on both their bodies was uncountable. They pounded, punched, kicked and slapped, with struggling arms and stony hearts. When their hands and legs began to tire, they would use their tails to twist each other's bodies and squeeze till bones cracked under the immense pressure. When even their tails got tired, they began to whirl around each other like mighty kites flying in the wind. Sugreeva's strength began to wane and Vali's strength was still as it was in the beginning. The pendant had done its job by draining Sugreeva and giving Vali half of his brother's strength. Sugreeva desperately began to look around for Rama. Where was his saviour? Would he break his promise and leave him to die? Hanuman and the others looked at Rama. He appeared absolutely calm.

Vali was now holding Sugreeva by his neck against a boulder. His demonic eyes revealed that he intended to end the match. Sugreeva struggled, his legs dangling, trying to free himself. The very next moment, Vali's shrill laughter dissipated into silence.

He staggered, let go of his hold on Sugreeva and fell backwards. Sugreeva was surprised. And relieved! And then he saw a golden arrow embedded in Vali's chest.

Vali was clueless as to what hit him. He struggled to remove the arrow and gave up after realising that everything was over now. But he still wanted to know which mighty warrior was capable of felling him. With one last effort, he pulled the arrow out and saw the name written on it. 'Rama'. Soon enough, Rama came and stood in front of him. Vali had only one question to ask him. Why did he shoot an innocent monkey from behind a tree? Without any malice or hatred, Rama explained to Vali all the things that he had done wrong. Kidnapping Sugreeva's wife was one reason. As a Kshatriya, it was Rama's duty to protect the innocent, which he did. Rama's promise to Sugreeva was another reason. Had he not been hiding, Vali might have surrendered and Rama's promise would have remained unfulfilled. More than anything else, Rama had vowed to offer shelter to anyone who surrendered to him. But if an offender like Vali surrendered to him, then he would have to let him go unpunished.

That wouldn't be right. When Rama offered these explanations, Vali, standing at the edge of life, asked for forgiveness. He called Sugreeva close and handed over the kingdom to him, ending all enmity between them. He handed over his son Angad to Rama for protection. And finally, he bade goodbye to his wife. It was time for him to leave. Sugreeva hugged his brother, feeling sorry for the tragic end.

13
Monkey Power

"Sita... Sita... Sita..." Seated in a lotus posture like an advanced yogi, Rama was absorbed in chanting the single-word mantra. More than a month had passed since Vali had been killed and Sugreeva was coronated king of Kishikandha.

Nothing could be done till the rainy season lasted. They simply had to endure the pain of separation from Sita, patiently waiting for the season to change. The chaturmasa or the four months of the rainy season were considered to be the time of sleep for the gods. Sugreeva had promised that he would galvanise his monkey army into action at the end of the four months. They would search every corner of the world to find Sita.

Rama was getting impatient to begin the search. Where was Sugreeva? Just then, Sugreeva entered Rama's cave and fell at his feet, apologising for the delay. Of course Sugreeva hadn't come out of gratitude. Hanuman's reminder and Laxman's warning had pushed him into action.

Sugreeva brought Rama out of the cave to show him a spectacle. Rama and Laxman glanced below the cliff. What an unbelievable scene it was. A massive army of millions of monkeys was standing below. Every inch of land was covered with monkeys. Wanting to introduce Rama to all his leaders, Sugreeva directed Rama's attention to each of the prominent leaders in the Vanara army, giving Rama a short introduction of each. Rama and Laxman were really impressed by the show of strength. They had never seen so many monkeys before. Each more impressive than the other. Some were leaders of crores of monkeys, some had tails that could slash their enemies. Some had mystical abilities to alter a person's state of mind, while others had shape-shifting abilities.

Amongst them was also a bear, Jambavan, the oldest living creature in the universe, only second to Lord Brahma.

For the first time in months, Rama smiled. With this kind of an army, it was impossible not to find Sita! Rama then requested Sugreeva to go ahead and organise the army to achieve their goals.

Sugreeva divided the army into four sections, one for each direction. East, west, north and south. For the southern direction, he reserved his best soldiers—Angad, Hanuman and Jambavan. He gave detailed instructions to each division on which routes they should take and which they should avoid, which are safe and which are not, to ensure maximum efficiency in the search for Sita. He ended by saying that if they did not come back in 30 days, he would kill them himself.

The troops left one by one. Rama dropped a glittering object into the palms of Hanuman. It was a golden ring studded with a precious large stone on top. "As soon as Sita sees the ring, she will know that you are my envoy," he explained. Hanuman safely tucked it away in his waist cloth.

"Sita not found!"

Sugreeva was highly upset when three divisions returned with negative reports. Turning to Rama, he said, "As long as Hanuman doesn't return, I won't lose hope."

Only half a day was left in the 30-day period.

Meanwhile, the monkey army led by Angad had also been wandering about without success. As the days passed and the terrain got tougher, the excitement began to wane. They had run out of water. Their minds were totally agitated. Boils dotted their soles.

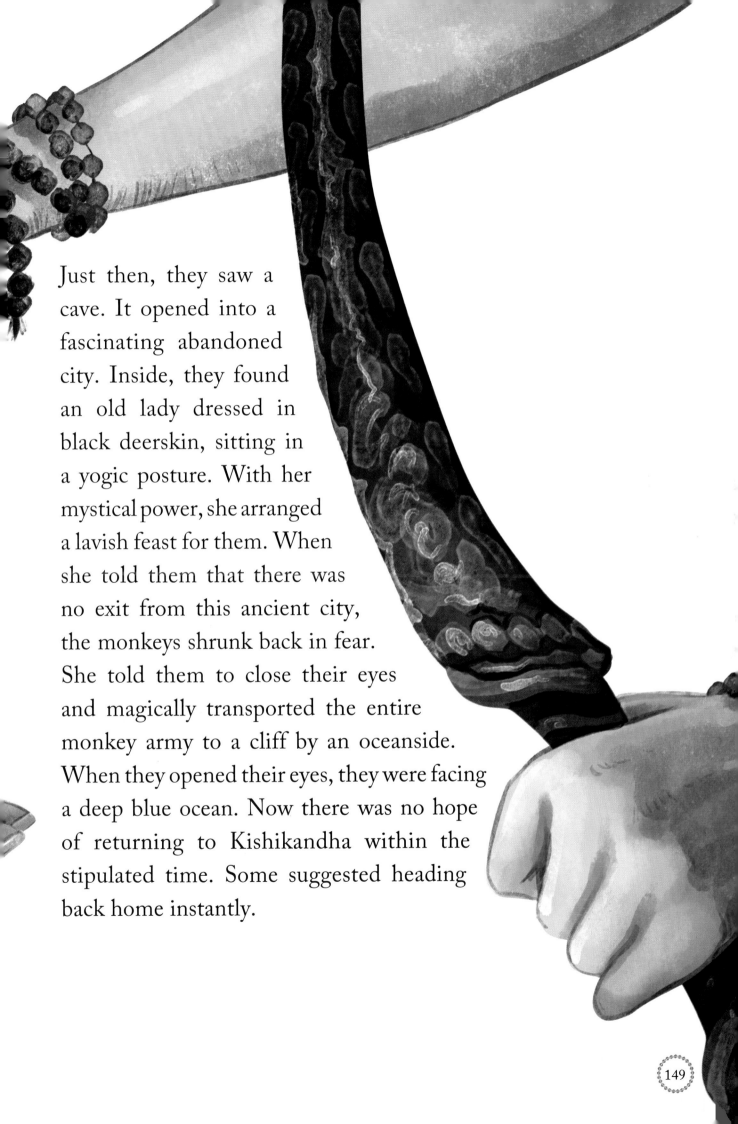

Just then, they saw a cave. It opened into a fascinating abandoned city. Inside, they found an old lady dressed in black deerskin, sitting in a yogic posture. With her mystical power, she arranged a lavish feast for them. When she told them that there was no exit from this ancient city, the monkeys shrunk back in fear. She told them to close their eyes and magically transported the entire monkey army to a cliff by an oceanside. When they opened their eyes, they were facing a deep blue ocean. Now there was no hope of returning to Kishikandha within the stipulated time. Some suggested heading back home instantly.

It was Hanuman's idea that in times of trouble like this, one should remember Rama. One of the monkeys wanted to hear the full story of Rama from him. With a smile on his face, Hanuman began narrating Lord Rama's story, right from the beginning.

Hours passed by as the monkeys heard about Lord Rama's enchanting life with rapt attention. "… Jatayu decided to fight Ravana despite knowing that he stood no chance against this mammoth demon… Jatayu sacrificed his life in order to protect Mother Sita." As soon as Hanuman said this, they heard a loud noise. SCHRRREEEEEECCHHHHHHH!

Hanuman looked up and at the edge of the cliff was the biggest vulture he had ever seen. Not just the biggest but also the most ferocious one ever known. But tears were flowing from his big moist eyes. Hanuman began to climb the cliff in order to speak to the vulture, for he was surely in great pain.

"Did I hear correctly? Did you mention that Jatayu is dea—?" While uttering the word 'dead', the vulture choked up and couldn't complete the sentence. Without saying a word, Hanuman nodded his head. The bird began to wail pitifully and said, "He was my brother. Jatayu was my younger brother and I am Sampati. We were separated from each other when we were children. I haven't seen him since then."

Hanuman also shared that they were having trouble finding Mother Sita. Sampati reassuringly said, "Do not worry. I will definitely help you locate Sita."

He just flew into the sky for a few minutes and came back with information. "I have some news for you! About 100 yojanas (an ancient measure of distance equal to approximately 80 miles) from here, right in the middle of the ocean lies a lavish island called Lanka. That's where Ravana has housed Sita. She is surrounded by fierce-looking rakshasa women. I recommend that only one of you venture to that place and ascertain the exact location of Sita."

Angad asked each of the monkeys for their best performance. One monkey said he could jump 10 yojanas. Another said 20. Another 50. 70. 80! Now everyone looked at Angad. He said, "I can jump 100! But then I will not be able to return due to fatigue." Jambavan began analysing the strengths and weaknesses of each monkey.

Hanuman was the only monkey who remained silent. Jambavan knew about his curse. Because he was very naughty as a child, a rishi had cursed him to forget all his powers till someone reminded him about them. Jambavan thought that it was the right time to remind Hanuman of his capabilities.

Jambavan inspired him to get into action. "Get up and leap across the ocean. The entire army is anxious to witness your prowess. Arise, O monkey hero Hanuman! Arise, O Pavana-putra Hanuman!"

As Jambavan spoke, Hanuman's confidence rose. He began to grow in size. Within moments, he was a few hundred feet tall. The other monkeys looked up in amazement at the sudden transformation of their friend. Hanuman began lashing his tail on the ground, creating tremors.

He ran towards Mount Mahendra, covering the distance in a few strides. Climbing the mountain in some steps, he reached the peak in a flash. Standing right at its summit, he yelled, "Victory to Lord Rama! Jai Shri Rama! Today itself I will find Sita and offer Lord Rama's ring to her and convey his message."

14

Hail Hanuman!

"Hurray! Come back soon!" The monkeys cheered and jumped as Hanuman took off in full glory. He waved to them as he surged ahead. Like a first-time traveller, he was both excited and nervous.

Soon, Hanuman saw something glittering in the ocean. What could it be? It was a radiant mountain rising from inside the ocean. The colossal mountain almost touched the skies and blocked Hanuman's path. He couldn't see a thing beyond the massive obstacle. Dotted with scenic lakes, fruit-bearing trees, healing herbs and beautiful gardens, the mountain looked like paradise. Right at the centre, almost at par with Hanuman's height, appeared a brilliantly effulgent personality who stood with folded hands.

"My dear hero, I am Mount Mainaka. Long back, all the mountains had wings. We could freely fly from one place to another. Unfortunately, because of a few proud mountains, Indra decided to clip all our wings, making us immobile. With the help of the ocean god, Varuna, I hid under the ocean. By serving you, I will get a chance to reciprocate the kindness Varuna had bestowed upon me ages ago. Kindly come and purify my peak with your saintly visit." An invitation to rest is always tempting. But not for Hanuman. Thanking the mountain, he said, "The word 'rest' does not feature in my dictionary when I am on a mission. I cannot think of my own comforts till I have achieved my goal. I must move on." Hanuman touched the mountain with his hands, accepting its service, and flew away.

Even though Hanuman was flying way above the ocean's surface, a fountain of water came flying up. Hanuman slowed down to determine the cause of the disturbance. With a huge splash emerged a gigantic demoness who had the face of a human but the trunk of a python. This was Surasa, the mother of the Nagas, in her most terrifying form.

She spoke, or rather hissed like a snake, "Hssss… I have Brahma'ssss boon that I can eat anyone who passsssses over me. Today, you are my food. No one can ssssssstop me now…" Surasa opened her mouth to devour Hanuman in one gulp. In order to save himself, Hanuman expanded himself a bit. Soon it became a competition with Surasa expanding herself and then Hanuman expanding himself further. When Hanuman was 10 yojanas in height, Surasa expanded her mouth to become 20-yojanas tall. Hanuman stretched more to reach 30 yojanas, while Surasa turned 40-yojanas tall. The tussle continued till Hanuman stopped at 80 and Surasa at 100 yojanas. In a flash, Hanuman shrunk himself to the size of a fly, dashed into her mouth and slid on her tongue. He glided all the way into her throat and entered her belly.

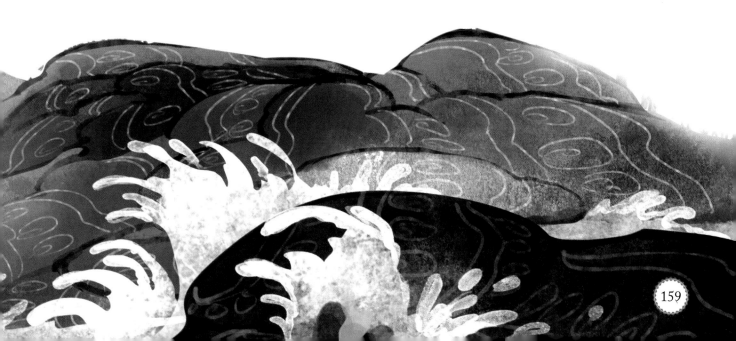

On reaching her belly, he flew up again, came out of her mouth and assumed his regular size. Surasa could feel something enter her mouth, reach her belly and exit. But, it all happened so fast that she hardly had any time to react. By then Hanuman had tricked her and already made his exit.

With folded hands, and a heart-warming voice, Hanuman said, "My dear mother, I have honoured the words of Lord Brahma. I have entered your belly and come out. Kindly bless me and permit me to proceed on my journey to find Mother Sita."

Blessing him profusely, she disappeared. A free Hanuman began to soar into the sky, yet again. This time, he hoped there would be no new obstacles. Time was running out and the pressure was mounting. Surasa had wasted sufficient time in competing with him unnecessarily. Suddenly, something went wrong and he wasn't able to move forward. He was suspended in thin air. Weird! It was as if someone had caught him, though no one was visible. In a flash, he was being dragged downwards. He had no idea what was happening and who was controlling his movements. Then he saw a shadow. It was his own shadow. Someone was holding it down. It struck him that an evil force was controlling it. He was still falling and soon he would hit the surface. He had to think fast. Without any warning, the calm surface of the water split and a huge monster emerged with her mouth wide open. Simhika! Hanuman recognised her immediately. She was the demoness Sugreeva had warned him about. She was the greatest obstacle for anyone who tried reaching Lanka. Her wide mouth was filled with countless razor-sharp teeth.

Instantly, Hanuman shrunk himself to the size of a fly and entered her mouth. Next, he extended both his hands and held them far out. As he slid into her throat, the ten fingers of his hands, which had sharp nails, began to slice through her organs. He systematically entered every corner of her body and ripped apart all the essential organs. Tearing open her stomach, he rushed out.

As soon as he flew out of her body, Simhika collapsed with blood pouring out from her mouth and ruptured stomach. Lanka was now only minutes away, but Sita still seemed hours away. The aerial view of Lanka was picturesque, lined with sparkling beaches and lush green forests. Landing on a mountaintop, Hanuman patiently waited for nightfall to execute his first move. Shrunk down to the size of a cat, he entered the golden city of Lanka.

"Who are you?" a voice roared while a huge javelin was aimed to block his onward movement. Little Hanuman was taken aback. Looking up, he saw a pair of dangerous-looking red eyes staring at him in anger. "No one enters Lanka without my sanction and King Ravana's permission. Since you dared the impossible, you have to face the consequences."

She quickly delivered a swift slap to Hanuman. No one had ever hit him like this! Outraged, he roared and hurled a blow that sent her reeling in pain. She fell at a distance with a thud, remaining immobile for a while.

When she got up, she had tears in her eyes. She wasn't the wild demoness anymore. With folded hands, she kneeled before Hanuman in supplication and said, "Long ago, Lord Brahma had told me that the day a monkey punches me, it would mark the beginning of the end of Lanka. Now, I know for sure that Ravana will soon be history. I bless you, may you achieve success in your mission. Lord Rama shall be victorious." He was pleasantly surprised to see the effect of his punch. He should punch more often maybe, he thought grinning wickedly. Could he open the gates of his luck with a punch as well? Because he needed luck to find Sita in such a huge and heavily guarded empire.

15

Torture in Ashoka Vatika

"Is this Sita?" Hanuman wondered aloud as his search led him to an Ashoka tree. Considering the description given to him by Rama, this had to be the Sita whom millions of monkeys were looking for. Her body was emaciated by months of fasting and her face was wet with rivers of tears running down her cheeks.

Surrounding her were hundreds of vicious one-eyed and one-eared demonesses. On counting closely, Hanuman realised they were 700 in total. Just then, a series of drumbeats startled everyone.

Hanuman hid behind the foliage of the tall tree he was seated on. Ravana walked in majestically.

"O Sita, accept me as your master. Forget that aimless, wandering fellow Rama. You know very well that he won't be able to find you, let alone rescue you," Ravana commanded and begged at the same time.

"Like sunlight is inseparable from the sun, Sita is inseparable from Rama," Sita said sternly.

Ravana was furious with Sita's attitude. She hadn't budged an inch even after months of being in captivity.

As the sun set again that day, some movement caught Hanuman's attention. When he glanced below, he was shocked to see what Sita was doing. She had tied her long hair to a tree branch and was looping it around her neck in an attempt to end her life. He began to panic. As he silently prayed for wisdom, he thought of a brilliant way to handle the situation.

In a sombre yet robust voice, he began to narrate the story of Rama. Right from his birth, to banishment, to exile, to Sita's abduction. As he spoke, Hanuman could see Sita slowly relaxing. By the time he finished, she had taken off the noose and was seated on the floor, below the tree, crying tears of joy. He jumped and landed right in front of her, assuming a miniature form. Hanuman produced the signet ring that Rama had given him. Glancing at that ring brought a flood of tears in Sita's eyes. She kept glancing at it with love, crying and smiling at the same time.

"My dear mother, kindly come with me. Sit on my back and I will take you to Rama immediately. All your misery will end in a few minutes."

Hanuman's words took Sita by surprise. How could a tiny monkey claim to carry her? Expanding himself till he was giant-sized, he kneeled before her on one leg with folded hands. Sita's jaw dropped when she saw that the tiny monkey had become much bigger than the tree she was sitting under. In the next instant, he again shrunk himself, resuming his normal size. Sita was reassured but still refused his offer and, instead, asked him the question that had been nagging her for the last few months. "How is Rama?"

"Rama has grown so thin now, that the signet ring I just gave you would fit his wrist like a bracelet."

"Flying across the ocean is not an easy task. If you have managed it, you surely must be as powerful as Garuda or Vayu," said Sita, appreciating Hanuman for his monumental achievement. "O divine mother, in the entire monkey army there is not even one monkey who is less than me in abilities. Rama has picked me for this errand of delivering a message to you because he considers me the lowest in the cadre and fit to be a messenger."

Sita was impressed with Hanuman's humility. She said, "I have seen you change sizes, so, I am confused; what is your real size?"

Hanuman was happy to hear Sita's enquiry. He humbly explained, "I am always small. But, by God's grace I can turn bigger in size when needed. God is big and his power is great, therefore, I can grow big by taking shelter in him. Otherwise, I am always small. I only request you to give me something that assures Lord Rama that I actually met the right person in Lanka."

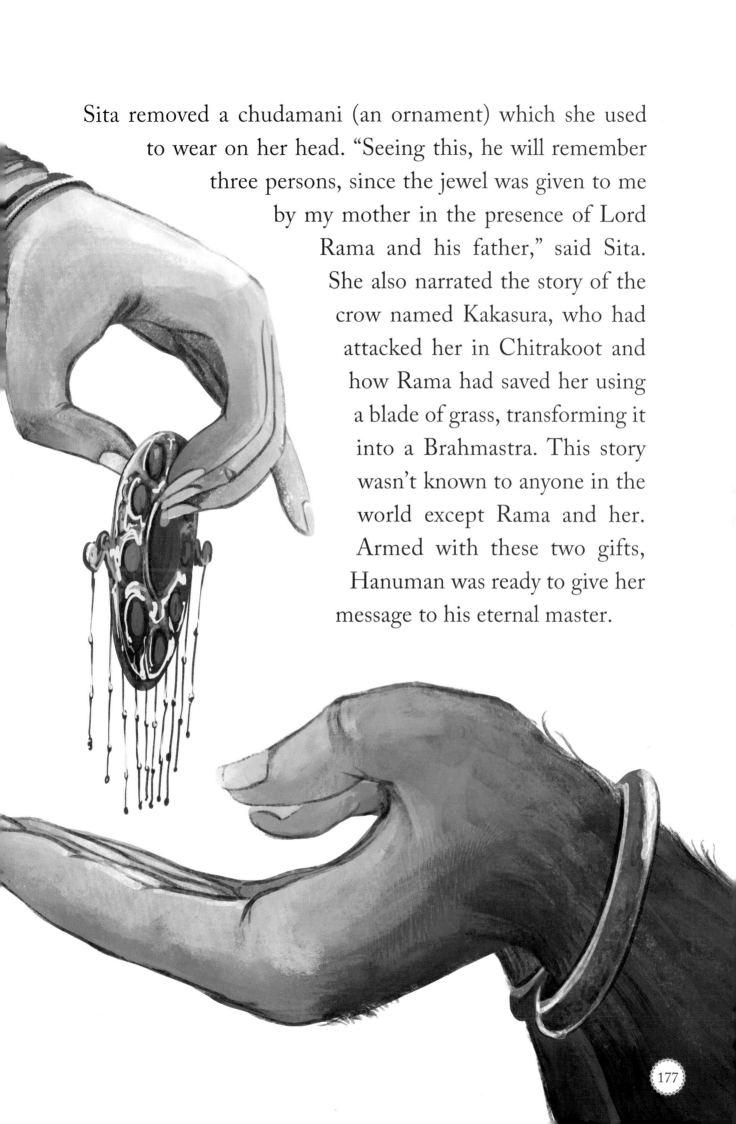

Sita removed a chudamani (an ornament) which she used to wear on her head. "Seeing this, he will remember three persons, since the jewel was given to me by my mother in the presence of Lord Rama and his father," said Sita. She also narrated the story of the crow named Kakasura, who had attacked her in Chitrakoot and how Rama had saved her using a blade of grass, transforming it into a Brahmastra. This story wasn't known to anyone in the world except Rama and her. Armed with these two gifts, Hanuman was ready to give her message to his eternal master.

16

A Hero Returns

"Holy smoke!" Ravana's soldiers exclaimed when they saw the entire Ashoka Vatika smouldering. Everything was destroyed. The once celebrated royal gardens of Lanka, the pride of their king, were nothing but a crematorium now. The only tree that was still standing was the Ashoka tree under which Sita was still seated. But where was the destroyer, they wondered. They spread out in ten directions to comb him out.

Hanuman was now standing on a thick branch of the Ashoka tree, with one hand on his hip and the other holding a mace on his shoulder. Seeing Hanuman's strong physique, the soldiers gasped. Thousands of soldiers began running towards him with raised weapons. Swinging his mace, Hanuman sent them back flying with all their limbs smashed. Each time he would shout out with joy, "Jai Shri Rama!"

Within a few minutes, all the 80,000 men were history. Hanuman merrily ate fruits till the next batch came. This time, Ravana sent his own son, the heroic Akshay Kumar, who had a track record of winning every battle. He tried his best to overpower the wild monkey prince, but nothing he did was even remotely effective.

Finally, Hanuman picked him up by his legs and spun him around several times before smashing him on the ground, crushing his head to pulp. The ghastly death of Akshay Kumar created waves of panic in Lanka.

With no other choice left, Ravana sent Indrajit—his eldest and most powerful son. Indrajit understood that the enemy was not an ordinary one. Killing him was out of question. He decided to use the most powerful and sure-shot weapon he had in his possession, the Brahma Pasha. As soon as the missile of Lord Brahma hit Hanuman's chest, he froze. He closed his eyes and allowed himself to be bound by the ropes of the Brahma Pasha. Lord Brahma had blessed him with a boon: no weapon could ever harm him. But, out of respect for the divine weapon and in order to meet Ravana, Hanuman allowed himself to be captured.

Seated on a raised emerald-studded throne of gold, Ravana looked down upon the wily monkey that had brought Lanka to a standstill. Since no one was offering him a seat, Hanuman coiled his tail behind his legs and created a seat for himself. Purposefully, he raised the seat so high that Ravana had to now look up at him.

Hanuman warned Ravana to return Sita with dignity, failing which a disaster awaited him. Hearing such arrogant words from this monkey, in his own court, Ravana screamed in rage, "Kill this monkey!" Vibhishan, the younger brother of Ravana, dissuaded him from harming a mere messenger. The code of conduct for warriors strictly forbade harming the messenger. Ravana decided not to kill Hanuman, but planned something worse.

Soon, hundreds of pieces of cloth were brought to the courtroom and wrapped around Hanuman's long tail. When stretched completely, his tail almost entirely covered the floor of the courtroom. Once the Herculean project of tying rags to the tail was completed, the tail was set ablaze. Hanuman was then taken all over the city to demonstrate to the people of Lanka that their criminal had been caught and was being punished. But Hanuman used this as an opportunity to take a guided tour of Lanka and study its security system. Deciding that it was time for action now, he shrunk himself and slipped out of the ropes that bound him. Only a piece of rope remained in the hands of the soldiers who were dragging him around. Surprised, they found him on the roof of a building. How in the world did he reach there? As they looked at him in dismay, the naughty Hanuman dipped his tail, setting the entire building on fire. Then he jumped to the roof of another building and set it on fire as well. Assuming a gigantic form, he jumped from one building to another, setting everything on fire. Except for Vibhishan's palace, soon, every other building was on fire. The golden city was burning!

Meanwhile, a disappointed and dejected Rama was still waiting for one person to return. Hanuman was his only hope. Suddenly, there was complete pandemonium. From the southern direction, hordes of monkeys were returning with Hanuman flying right above them. Just then, he heard something he couldn't believe. At the top of his voice, Hanuman shouted, "Found Sita I!" Hanuman was not just intelligent, but also sensitive beyond comprehension. He had actually distorted language to give joy to Rama. The only word that would revive Rama's hope and give him the impetus to hold on till Hanuman reached him was 'found'. There was nectar filled in that one word, so what if it was grammatically wrong.

Hanuman brought out the chudamani given to him by Sita and handed it over to a teary-eyed Rama. Memories of his beloved came flooding back to him.

Hanuman also narrated the episode of Kakasura that Sita had shared with him. Seeing Sita's chudamani and hearing the story of Kakasura, Rama knew beyond doubt that Hanuman had indeed met Sita. "Hanuman, you have saved not only Sita's life but also my life!" He pulled Hanuman close to his heart and embraced him lovingly. Hanuman closed his eyes and savoured every moment of that embrace.

Bridging Two Hearts

"Hurray!" Sugreeva was greeted with cries of jubilation when he announced that they would now begin the journey to Lanka to rescue Mother Sita. There was hope and excitement in the air. The monkeys would occasionally carry Rama and Laxman on their shoulders so that they could march even more quickly.

Their enthusiasm multiplied with each passing second. The most interesting thought on each monkey's mind was how he would kill Ravana. Upon reaching Mount Mahendra at the shore of the ocean, they again faced the same problem. How would the army cross this vast ocean? Rama called for a meeting of all monkey chiefs to get their suggestions.

At the same time, Ravana had convened a meeting with his ministers after learning that Rama was preparing to cross the ocean to attack Lanka. "We will destroy the monkey army!" the foolish ministers boasted, forgetting the fact that a single monkey had succeeded in burning Lanka. While all his ministers glorified him, predicting an easy victory for Ravana, it was only his younger brother Vibhishan who went against the flow and advised Ravana to return Sita and ask for forgiveness. "Kidnapping Sita was a sin to begin with," he explained. Ravana, unable to bear Vibhishan's words, threw him out of the kingdom.

With no desire to stay in Lanka, Vibhishan zoomed up into the sky and proceeded to the spot where Rama and Laxman were camping with their army. All of a sudden, the monkeys saw a glow in the sky coming towards them. "I am sure this is a rakshasa coming from Lanka," said Sugreeva. All the monkeys wanted to attack the evil force right away. Having heard the monkeys, Vibhishan folded his hands and said, "I am Vibhishan, brother of Ravana. I tried to convince him to give up his sinful acts and return Sita, but he only insulted me publicly and threw me out of the kingdom. Rama is my only shelter now. Please take me to him."

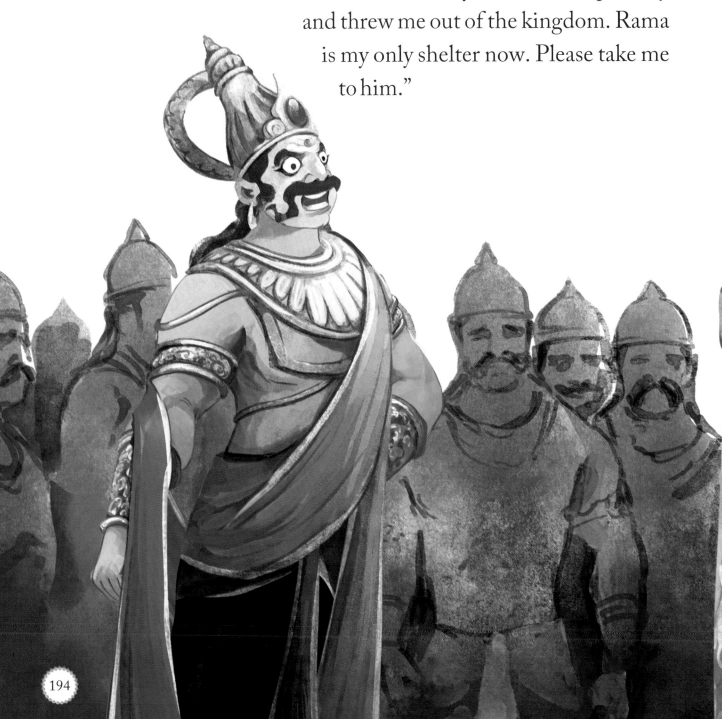

Sugreeva was sceptical. How could Ravana's brother be trusted? He was from the enemy camp. Trusting him could be fatal to their mission. Sugreeva conveyed his thoughts to Lord Rama, "I believe this rakshasa has been sent by Ravana himself. If we give him shelter, he could betray us and leak our strategies to Ravana. Let us kill him now itself."

Rama said, "Your fears are totally justified. What do the others say?" Angad, Jambavan and other monkey leaders were also reluctant to trust Vibhishan blindly. Now, it was Hanuman's turn to speak. He said, "It is not surprising that Vibhishan has come. It was he who directed me to Ashoka Vatika to find Sita. He is the only person in Lanka who chants the holy name of Rama. He has honestly stated why he is here. There is nothing strange. He knows all of Ravana's secrets and can be an asset for us."

Hanuman quietly added one more line that made Rama very happy, "A doctor does not choose which patient to cure and which not to. He gives medicine to everyone who comes to him."

Rama announced his decision, "When one seeks my shelter, I cannot refuse. Even if Ravana comes asking for shelter, I will accept him. This is my dharma. Even if I have to suffer, I will never deviate from my duty." Rama welcomed Vibhishan into his camp with open arms. He addressed him as the king of Lanka and Vibhishan pledged his unending loyalty to Rama.

It was time to cross the ocean. On Vibhishan's suggestion, they first prayed to the ocean god to allow them to cross the ocean. After three days of praying, when the ocean god did not respond, Rama's eyes glowed with anger and he roared, "Laxman, bring my bow and arrow. I will dry up the ocean today for his arrogance."

Scared of Lord Rama's punishment, the ocean god came out of the water and clarified, "I am governed by the laws of nature. How can I change myself to allow passage to your army? Can water become stone? So, please forgive me for my inaction. But I can do one thing. I can hold all the rocks and boulders that your army throws. I will put it all in place to build a bridge."

Rama accepted the ocean god's offer as well as apology. Thus began the massive project of bridge construction. It was a marvellous piece of engineering in which every animal participated. Shouting with excitement, the monkeys and bears carried every rock, every boulder they could find to build the bridge, stone by stone. Some monkeys flew here and there to carry bigger rocks. Hanuman himself brought mountains from far-off places. It was a difficult job and time-consuming too.

Thousands of animals worked day and night. Also busy was a tiny little squirrel, carrying pebbles and sand from the shore and dropping them into the sea. So tiny was she that no one really noticed her until she happened to come in the way of a bigger monkey, who nearly tripped and fell on her. On discovering the squirrel below, he said, "Little squirrel, you are in the way. Move aside and allow us to work." The squirrel explained that she was also working for the same mission, building the bridge for Rama. Hearing her, all the monkeys had a hearty laugh. Compared to the mighty monkeys, what help could a little squirrel be? "Do you think you can build a bridge with pebbles? Rama has a big army to do that. Go home now!" the monkey chastised her. "I will not!" defied the squirrel, "I want to help Rama too."

Angered by the little squirrel's audacity, the monkey picked her up by the tail and flung her afar. The poor squirrel cried out Lord Rama's name in the air and landed in the palm of Rama himself, who had been quietly watching this interaction. He said, "O monkeys, you are doing a great job, but do not make fun of the small and weak. Her pebbles and sand will help bridge the gaps between stones. In addition, more important than what you do is the devotion and love with which you do it."

"This little squirrel here has immense devotion in her heart." The monkeys were ashamed of themselves. "A project is never completed by important people alone, they need the support of everyone. Every small effort counts and should be appreciated." The monkeys then invited the squirrel back to the task at hand. Construction was soon completed with the joint efforts of every animal, big and small. Carrying Rama and Laxman on their shoulders, the monkey army then crossed the bridge. In Lanka, a sepoy heard a crunch emanating from within the foliage of a tree. He went closer to inspect properly. Suddenly, he was hit by a half-eaten apple.

He was disgusted. Before he could even recover, a leg appeared and kicked him hard on his ribs. The sepoy went flying and landed on the ground. He died on the spot. Hanuman was now standing on a thick branch of the tree, with one hand on his hip and the other holding a mace on his shoulder. Seeing Hanuman's strong physique, the soldiers gasped. Lunging forward, he jumped down and kicked two soldiers on their heads, killing them instantly.

Thousands of soldiers began running towards Hanuman with raised weapons. Swinging his mace, Hanuman single-handedly sent them all back flying and flailing. Each time he would shout out with joy, "Jai Shri Rama!"

Ravana Falls

"Whoa! What a beautiful sight!" Exclaimed Rama, marvelling at the aerial view of Lanka from a mountaintop. On arriving at Lanka, he had first sent Angad as a messenger of peace. But the offer had only fuelled Ravana's anger and his rakshasas attacked Angad. Angad returned and Rama was now ready to assault Lanka, having surrounded it from all sides.

Shouting "Victory to Rama and Laxman" the monkeys rushed to attack as soon as they received their war signal. Some hurled big boulders and others uprooted big trees to attack the demons. Ravana's army was no less. They fought tooth and nail and soon there were thousands dead on each side. With maces clashing in the air and chariots falling apart, the deadly war continued. With his most heavyweight generals already dead, Ravana decided to wake his brother Kumbhakaran, who slept for six months and woke up for a day, only to sleep again for six months. Kumbhakaran was the strongest of all demons. This was an emergency and Ravana needed all the help possible.

Kumbhakaran had to be roused by beating drums, blowing conches, walking elephants over him and striking him with blunt weapons. Mountains of food were kept ready, which he would devour on waking. After he was sufficiently awake and well fed, he met Ravana and asked, "Brother, what can I do for you? Who do you want killed?"

Relieved to have Kumbhakaran by his side, Ravana told him all about Rama and his powerful army destroying their beautiful Lanka. Although Kumbhakaran was angry with Ravana for stupidly kidnapping Sita, his love for his brother was stronger. The tall and mighty Kumbhakaran rushed to the battlefield to destroy whoever dared to attack his brother. At the sight of this fearsome rakshasa, all the monkeys scattered to hide themselves. The brave ones fought with rocks and trees. But they were simply mosquitoes for the gigantic rakshasa, who only had to flick his wrists to end their lives. He rendered Angad unconscious and trapped Sugreeva in his arms. Joyous at capturing the king of monkeys, Kumbhakaran wanted to show off his trophy to Ravana. Like a wild beast, Sugreeva nibbled on his ears and nose. Taken by surprise, the demon loosened his hold on Sugreeva and he quickly escaped. Unable to return to Lanka, looking ugly and deformed, the demon backtracked to the enemy camp. None of the monkeys were any match for him. They climbed on him to scratch him with their sharp nails, but in vain.

Rama's blessed arrows had also failed to stop him. Taking aim with stronger, deadlier arrows, Rama first cut off his arms and legs and then beheaded the monstrous body of Kumbhakaran. Ravana was quickly informed that his brother's head had come flying into Lanka, while his body had fallen into the sea. Kumbhakaran's sons had also been slain. Ravana swooned with grief and utter disbelief. His brother was... dead? For a moment, he regretted starting the war.

His son Indrajit comforted him and said, "I'm still alive! No need to worry, father." He stepped onto the battlefield with great pomp, but the monkeys cheered in joy as their prince, Angad destroyed Indrajit's chariot. Along with his chariot, Indrajit lost his temper as well. He made himself invisible and showered arrows from the sky, killing many monkeys. Inspired, he shot serpent-darts at Rama and Laxman. The serpents tied both of them, felling them unconscious in the battlefield.

Garuda timely rescued the brothers by eating the serpents. The Lankan army rejoiced prematurely, while the monkey army patiently waited for their heroes to resurrect. Rama recovered in a couple of hours but Laxman remained unconscious. It was Hanuman's quick dash for medicinal herbs that revived Laxman. The fight resumed with Laxman determined to end Indrajit's role in the clash. It was a battle of equals that went on for many days. Finally, Laxman used the fatal Indra-astra to sever Indrajit's head from his body.

This bad news rattled Ravana to his bones. With fire fuming from his mouth and tears rolling from eyes, he grieved like never before. His entire support system had collapsed with the loss of Indrajit, the valiant conqueror of Indra. Ravana had underestimated the enemy and his plan had horribly backfired. With no weapons other than sticks and stones, the enemy had destroyed his entire army. Despite this realisation, he had still not learned his lesson. It was now or never. Left without any options, he decided to make an appearance himself. Disregarding evil omens like beasts crying and an unpredicted eclipse, he drove to the battlefield against the good advice of his wife. He triumphed past Rama's beastly defences and came face to face with Laxman. He overcame him and marched ahead to challenge Rama. The two warriors fought even from a distance, determined to slay each other using potent weapons and secret powers. Rama continuously shot arrows at his limbs, but the gigantic rakshasa stood tall. Laxman and Vibhishan too had recovered and were foiling all of Ravana's attempts to reach Rama. Determined to overcome the two, he shot a deadly arrow at Laxman.

Before he knew it, Laxman was unconscious on the ground. Unaware of this setback, Rama continued showering arrows on Ravana. Meanwhile, the monkeys took advice from a vaidya (a herbal doctor), who prescribed the lifesaving herb, sanjeevani. Hanuman dashed all the way to the Himalayas, brought the herb and helped revive Laxman. Much to everyone's delight, Laxman arose appearing stronger and more radiant than before. Until now, Rama had fought without as much as a chariot. Realising that this put Rama at a disadvantage, Indra sent his own chariot for him. Rama accepted it graciously. Then began a royal battle. With each side hurling powerful weapons, the duel went on and on. Though Rama had severed all of Ravana's ten heads, they had sprung up again. No matter how many times he cut the heads, they would always regenerate. The entire battlefield was covered with Ravana's heads, but he was still alive.

Rama looked at Vibhishan enquiringly. The demon's brother pointed to Ravana's belly button, suggesting that they attack his point of weakness. Rama did exactly that. The flaming arrow pierced Ravana's abdomen and he fell lifelessly on the ground. Flowers rained from heaven, celebrating the end of the most evil demon ever. Vibhishan did the last rites with a heavy heart. Ravana was, after all, his brother.

19

The Journey Home

Rama was impatient to inform Sita that Ravana was dead and that she had been rescued. He instructed Hanuman to take Vibhishan's permission to enter the palace grounds and give Sita the news. Following his instructions, Hanuman reached Ashoka Vatika. Sita was overjoyed to see him again and hear his message. She was extremely grateful to Hanuman for his humility, his wisdom and his service to her and Rama. "No one can match what you have done," she said tearfully. But Hanuman was not done yet. The 700 demonesses who had tortured his worshippable Mother Sita were still alive. "Mother, give me permission to slay these women who have tortured you. Why should they live?"

"What is their fault, dear son? They only obeyed the orders of their wicked master. Now that they have a new master, they will follow his orders. It is not right to punish them. Moreover, noble souls like you ought to show compassion to sinners as well as pious people."

Sita's kindness for all living entities touched Hanuman's heart. She was truly the ideal mother. Sita nudged Hanuman out of his reverie and asked him to take her out of Ashoka Vatika, to where her dear Rama was. Together, the two hurried out.

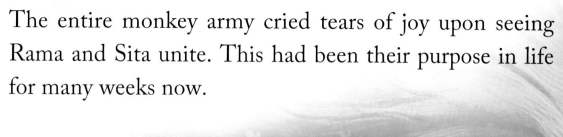

The entire monkey army cried tears of joy upon seeing Rama and Sita unite. This had been their purpose in life for many weeks now.

Mission impossible had been achieved. Rama asked Vibhishan if he could borrow the Pushpak Viman, because he had run out of time. If he did not reach Ayodhya the day his 14 years of exile ended, then Bharat would jump into the fire. He had not a moment to lose. He had to reach Ayodhya before Bharat lost hope. Vibhishan quickly called for his flying chariot and requested Rama to allow him to accompany them to Ayodhya for Rama's coronation. Rama as happy to have him aboard. And so, Rama, Laxman, Sita, Vibhishan, Hanuman and Sugreeva, along with millions of monkeys, boarded the Pushpak Viman. It was not an ordinary plane. It could magically increase or decrease in size to accommodate as many passengers as needed. As they took off, a cheer went up from the crowd.

Rama was busy showing Sita all the places they had crossed in this tumultuous journey. "This is where we landed in Lanka... This is the bridge the monkeys built to cross the vast ocean..." And so on. Blissful in the company of loved ones, Sita hung on to every word. "This is Kishikandha, where we first met Hanuman and Sugreeva." "Stop! Stop! Stop the plane!" Sita yelled as soon as she heard the word 'Kishikandha'. Everyone in the plane, including Rama, got scared. They asked, "What happened? Why do you want to stop?"

"I want all the monkey-women to come with us to Ayodhya. It is the least we can do for them. Let us pick them up too," she said smiling at the thought. There was very little time, but her request could not be refused. The monkeys were exhilarated at the thought of being united with their families and going to Ayodhya together. They marvelled at how sensitive Sita was and how much she thought about the happiness of others The plane landed and soon, millions of monkey-women had jumped on board. The excited chattering reached a crescendo with all the monkeys exchanging news and gossip with each other.

227

Sita looked gleefully at all of them and Rama looked fondly at Sita. It felt like one big family. She was so happy after a long time. The next stopover was Chief Guha's kingdom. Rama felt obligated to meet all those who had helped him in the last 14 years. Worried that he may not reach Ayodhya on time, he sent Hanuman ahead to inform Bharat that he was on his way. At least that would prevent Bharat from giving up his life. Hanuman took off in a jiffy. In Nandigram, at the outskirts of Ayodhya, he was greeted by a heart-rending sight. Bharat, who had become pale and sickly in Rama's absence, was standing in front of a burning pyre, ready to jump.

Since the stipulated time was nearly up and there was no sign of Rama, no word from him, why should he not end his life? Rama had not kept his word. Now, Hanuman was in a dilemma. What should he say? "Each time a problem arose, I was saved by the Rama Katha," he thought aloud. And so, sitting on a tree, Hanuman devotionally started singing the glories of Rama, starting from the beginning, to the part where he was now, on the way to Ayodhya. On hearing this wonderful song, hope surged within Bharat's heart. He looked for the divine singer and welcomed him. After giving Rama's message to Bharat and saving his life, Hanuman flew back to Rama.

When Hanuman entered Ayodhya again, with Rama this time, the entire city was dotted with lamps. Everything and everyone in Ayodhya was waiting for Rama's arrival with a song in their heart. The lamp flames seemed to be jumping in anticipation.

The trees were bent to shower their flowers. The birds and animals were standing with their ears alert, waiting to hear Rama's voice. The royal palace was decorated like a bride and music floated in every street, every corner, heralding the arrival of their Lord again.

Rama entered with his entourage and hugged each and every citizen. He personally met everyone and thanked them for their love and blessings.

Sage Vashishtha coronated him while Bharat remained at his feet, shedding tears of joy. Their father's wish had been fulfilled and Bharat was free from the burden of ruling the kingdom.

He wished that the moment never comes to an end...

The End